Are You My Sister?

Are You My Sister?
Copyright © 2023 by Cheri LePage

Published in the United States of America
ISBN   Paperback: 978-1-960629-81-4
ISBN   eBook: 978-1-960629-82-1

All rights reserved. No part of this publication may be reproduced, stored in a retrieval system or transmitted in any way by any means, electronic, mechanical, photocopy, recording or otherwise without the prior permission of the author except as provided by USA copyright law.

The opinions expressed by the author are not necessarily those of ReadersMagnet, LLC.

ReadersMagnet, LLC
10620 Treena Street, Suite 230 | San Diego, California, 92131 USA
1.619. 354. 2643 | www.readersmagnet.com

Book design copyright © 2023 by ReadersMagnet, LLC. All rights reserved.

Cover design by Ericka Obando
Interior design by Daniel Lopez

Are You My Sister?

Cheri LePage

ReadersMagnet, LLC

PROLOGUE
March 1987

Again, the day was a cool and rainy one. It was the third day in a row that Mariah, Whitney, Lindsay, and Lesley, the four Arrington sisters, had to stay in the house because of the weather. Mariah was going crazy and wanted to scream, as she was tired of her three younger sisters always tagging behind her. What nine-year-old girl wanted a seven—year old and a set of five-year-old twin sisters trailing after them wherever they went? They even followed her to the bathroom for heaven sakes. Her mother, Pam, was always telling her to watch after her sisters, so it fell on Mariah's young shoulders to keep her sisters from bothering their mother or waking up their father. Pam was a writer of science fiction romance books and needed time alone to write, and her father, Erik, worked nights, and needed a quiet house so he could sleep during the day.

On that rainy day, her sisters were being a bigger pain than usual, especially the twins. "I hate all of you.

I wish you would just go away and leave me alone," she screamed at them. "Go find someone else to pester."

"Mariah," her mother called out angrily, stomping into the room. "What is going on here?"

"I hate being the big sister," she bellowed. "I just want to play by myself, but I can't because I have to watch after these brats," she screamed pointing at her sisters. Then she ran into her room and slammed the door.

A few minutes later, Pam entered her room. "What do you have to say for yourself?"

"Mommy, I'm sorry," she muttered, fighting against her tears.

"Mariah, one day you may regret hating your sisters. How would you feel if one day you woke up to find your sisters had been taken away from you?"

"I don't hate them. I just don't want them tagging after me everywhere I go."

"Your sisters look up to you. Go apologize to them, then I'll pop some popcorn and we can play a game together," she said, brushing the hair out of Mariah's eyes.

She gave her mother a tight hug. "I love you, Mommy."

"I love you too. Tomorrow, we'll go school shopping, then go and out to lunch."

"That sounds like fun."

The next day was a happy day as the six Arringtons had a rare family outing together. When they got home, the girls put on their church dresses and her father took a picture of the four Arrington sisters, side by side. Her mother made duplicates of the picture so each of them could have their own copy. For Mariah, it was one of the happiest days in her life, but sadly, it was the last family outing for the Arrington family.

A week later, Mariah realized something was wrong when her father came home early from work. It wasn't until after she was in bed, and overheard her parents arguing that she realized her father had lost his job. When she got up the next morning, and her father wasn't at the breakfast table, she wondered where he could be.

"Mommy, where's Daddy?" she asked, thinking maybe he was still in bed.

"He had to leave," Pam said, refusing to look at her.

After breakfast, their mother drove them to their elementary school as usually. Since Lesley was going to the hospital to have her tonsils out, she remained in the car as her three sisters got out. Pam kissed each of three girls, good-bye, telling each of them she loved them. When Mariah she saw the tears in her mother's eyes, she knew something was wrong, but when she saw her friend Janet; she completely forgot to ask her mother why she was sad, as she ran to join her friend.

* * *

"Mr. Thurn, here are the folders on the new children that have been assigned to us. I have their suitcases with some of their belongings at my desk." Sabrina Minchew told her superior.

"Who are they?" Terrance Thurn asked, wondering if one of these children would be the one, he was looking for.

"They're three sisters who recently lost their parents."

"Thank you, Sabrina. Just set the files in my inbox and I'll get to them in a minute."

Sabrina put the folders down where he'd requested, and then left the room.

Terrance picked up the first folder. When he opened it and looked down at the picture of four sisters standing side by side, he was puzzled to why he didn't have a folder on the fourth child. He quickly frowned, when he realized she must have died with her parents. How sad.

He moved the picture aside and quickly read the printout about her. After seeing that she was the oldest sister, he put the folder down on his desk, and picked up the second folder, and read it. Still not happy with what he was seeing, he put it down and picked up the third folder. As he started reading, a smile covered his face. The information sheet on her said her name was Lindsay Arrington, she was five years old, and her two sisters were the only family she had left. This was just the child he'd been searching for him and his wife. As soon as he finished reading, he sat the folder down, picked up the phone, and dialed a number.

"Hello?" a female answered.

"Honey, I've found her," he said excitedly. "Her name is Lindsay and she's five years old."

"When can you bring her home?" Margie Thurn asked animatedly, clinching the phone to her ear.

"I'll bring her this evening when I come home."

"I'll get her room ready," she said excitedly. "I can't believe it. We're finally going to have a child of our own."

Terrance was surprised when his wife didn't ask any questions about the child but was relieved that he didn't have to tell her that she had two sisters who needed to be adopted as well. As Margie would have been upset if she had known that, but they had decided some time ago that they wanted just one child, a child who was old enough to start school, but young enough that they would forget about their old family.

He took the picture of Lindsay with her sisters out of her file folder and stuck it into the shredder, destroying her last connection of her family. After he did that, he returned to second child's file and slowly reread it. She was seven years old and would be perfect for what he had in mind. He went to the filing cabinet, and began searching it, quickly finding the file on a couple who were looking for a child just about her age. They only wanted one child and they didn't want to separate siblings. Therefore, he would be sure not to mention the child's remaining sister to them, then he picked up the phone and dialed the number written down in the folder.

"Hello?"

"Mr. O'Rourke, this is Terrance Thurn at Little Sheppard Home. I have good news for you. I've a seven-year little girl who has recently lost her family and needs a home. Are you interested?"

"When can we see her?" he asked eagerly.

"I'm having someone pick her up from school and she should be here in about an hour. Will that be soon enough for you?"

"That will be perfect. Thank you for thinking of us," Theo O'Rourke said breathlessly.

"You're welcome. I'll see you in an hour." He disconnected the line, then dialed another number.

"Hello?"

"Bianca, this is Terrance Thurn. I have a special job for you."

"What is it?" Bianca Hurst asked him, knowing it would have something to do with a child.

"I have a child I need for you to retrieve for me."

"Give me the child's name and location," she said, while in the back of her mind, she was thinking that this would be the last child for her. It was time for her to start looking for a new job, one that didn't entail children and their lost families.

Terrance quickly gave her Whitney name and the address of the school. "I'd like for the child to be here in less than an hour if possible."

"I'll go get her now."

"She has two sisters at the same school, and I would prefer she doesn't see either of them."

"I understand. I'll do my best that she doesn't see them." She hated the thought that the three sisters would probably never see each other ever again.

"Thank you." He hung up the phone, then picked up the first folder again, opened it up and looked down at her picture. She was a cute little girl, but because of her age, he felt it would be hard to find someone to adopt her, then checked his files until he found an opening in a foster home. It wasn't a perfect place for her, but it would have to do for now. He picked up the phone and called his assistant.

"Yes, Mr. Thurn," Sabrina responded.

"I need for you to send two people to the school, one to pick up Mariah Arrington and one to get her sister, Lindsay and bring them both here."

"What about third girl?" she asked.

"I've already sent someone to pick her up."

"Why not have just one person get all three of them?" she asked innocently, not thinking that something shady could be going on regarding these precious children.

"Because this is the way I want this done," he replied sternly.

"Yes, sir. I'll see to it immediately." Siblings were usually kept together, so Sabrina couldn't understand why Mr. Thurn would want the three girls retrieved separately. Was he planning to separate the girls and send them to different homes? It wasn't really any of her business, but she felt something dishonest might be into play here.

After Terrance finished the call, he phoned the woman at the foster home to inform her that someone would be bringing her another child later today. The woman seemed extremely too happy about having another child in her care, and he figured she was seeing dollars signs instead of a homeless orphan who needed a home, but he really didn't care.

Then he called the girls school to explain the situation to the principal, telling her that the three girls would be picked up separately. When he was done with his call, he took the pictures out of the other folders and put one in each of the two remaining suitcases.

* * *

MARIAH

Just after lunch, Helen Ackerman, the principal, came to Mariah's classroom and asked her to come to her office with her. Once there, she told her that both of her parents had been killed. Mariah was shocked at the news, then the realization of what the loss of her parents meant, and she began crying.

Helen tried to comfort her, telling her that she was going to live at a special home for children who had lost their families. When Mariah asked where her sisters were, the principal said she had been informed that someone was coming to get them separately and assumed they would be taken to a different foster home. Mariah cried as the principal's words sunk in, she'd finally gotten her wish, her sisters were now out of her life.

A woman came into the room and introduced herself as Terri Thompson, telling her that she was there to take her to her new home. Mariah told Terri that she wanted to go to her parents' funeral, but Terri told her that wasn't possible, and wondered why she wasn't with her sisters at a time like this. Mariah was saddened to know that she wouldn't even get to see her sisters one last time to tell them she loved them. When they arrived at Little Sheppard Home, Terri took her to Terrance's office and knocked on his door.

"Come in."

"Mr. Thurn, this is Mariah Arrington."

"Come in child," he said pleasantly, then turned to Terri. "Thank you for bringing her to me."

"You're welcome." Terri looked over at Mariah. "I hope things go well for you." She nodded at Mariah and then left the room.

"Mariah, I'm Mr. Thurn, I'm sorry that you have to be here."

"I want to be with my sisters."

"I'm sorry, but that won't be possible. You'll be staying in a foster home until you're adopted or until you're eighteen. I have some of your belongings for you to take with you." He handed her a suitcase, telling her it was time for her to leave for her new home.

When she arrived at what would be her home for the next year, she opened her suitcase, but other than some of her clothes, the only other item in it, was the picture of her with her sisters. Each night she cried herself to sleep, regretting her words to her mother about hating her sisters.

She hated the foster home she was taken to and it never felt like home to her. She met with several prospected parents during the first few months, but no one wanted her when they desired a baby or younger child.

When she was ten, Ned and Vera Faber, a middle age couple who didn't have any other children, adopted her. They were wonderful parents, but Mariah still missed her own family, especially her sisters. Her life now was with Ned and Vera, and she forced herself to accept that she would never see her Whitney, Lindsay, and Leslie again. The years passed, but Mariah never forgot her sisters.

* * *

WHITNEY

Whitney kissed her mother good-bye, then took hold of Lindsay's hand, and went into the school to take her sister to her classroom. An hour later, Mrs. Ackerman came into her classroom asking for her, and she instantly knew something wrong by the sad expression on the principal's face. Neither of them spoke as they walked down the hall, but once they were in her office, Whitney found out that her parents had died. When she asked about her sisters, Mrs. Ackerman just shook her head and told her she was sorry, but she didn't know anything except that Mariah had already be taken away and someone would be coming by later for Lindsay.

Bianca Hurst came into the room and told her that she was taking her to her back to office. When they arrived at the office, Bianca took her to Mr. Thurn's office, stopping at his assistant's desk.

"I've brought Whitney Arrington to see him."

"I'll tell Mr. Thurn that she's here."

The next few hours went by quickly for Whitney. She was introduced to Terrance Thurn, and he explained to her that Theo and Peggy O'Rourke were going to be her new parents. She wanted to ask about her sisters, but the man made her uncomfortable. She was introduced to Theo and Peggy O'Rourke, then they took her to their home, and she cried all the way there.

After Whitney was settled in her new room, she asked where her sisters were and when she was going to see them. It was then that Peggy explained that her sisters were dead.

"I don't understand. That isn't what Mrs. Ackerman told me. How could Mariah and both of the twins be dead?"

"I don't know the details. I only know that all your family was killed," Peggy told her gently.

"But Lindsay was going to the hospital, and my other two sisters were in class when they took me away. How could they be dead?" she argued. "I was told they were being sent to other homes."

"Whitney, the man at the adoption agency was very hush hush about your situation, but he did tell my husband that all your family was deceased. I'm sorry this has happened to you, but Theo and I will try to be good parents to you."

And they were. It wasn't easy for her, but she slowly started to heal over the loss of her family, and she came to love her new parents. But in the back of her mind, Whitney knew her sisters were out there somewhere, and when she got older, she was going to look for them.

* * *

LINDSAY

Mrs. Ackerman came to Lindsay's classroom and told her that she needed to speak with her. Why did the principal want to talk to her? Lindsay was terrified she was going to be punished for something she'd done wrong, but she knew she had been a good girl.

"Lindsay, you aren't in trouble. I just need to talk to you without your classmates."

The two were quiet as they walked to the principal's office.

"Now sit down in that chair there." She pointed to a small chair next to an adult-sized chair, then she sat down next to Lindsay and picked up one of her hands. "I'm sorry to tell you this, but I've bad news for you."

Lindsay tightened the grip on Mrs. Ackerman's hand. "I'm ready," she responded bravely.

Mrs. Ackerman sadly told Lindsay about the death of her parents, as well as informing her that she would be going to a foster house to live until she was adopted or until she was eighteen.

"What? Where are Mariah and Whitney?"

"There are already gone to their new homes."

"I want my mommy," she cried.

Mrs. Ackerman pulled the five—year old into her arms. "I'm so sorry." A knock interrupted whatever else she was going to say. "Come in."

"I've come for the other child," Sabrina told her.

Lindsay left with the woman she didn't know, crying at the empty feeling in her chest, she was scared and distress over the loss of her family.

When they arrived, Sabrina took her to Terrance's office. "You sit right here," she told her pointing to a chair in front of Terrance's desk. "Mr. Thurn wants to talk to you."

Lindsay just nodded as she sat down in the chair, then watched as the man stood. Panic filled her as her eyes took in the size of the large man, a man who was so much larger than her father was. Tears started down her cheeks, petrified of what he was going to do to her.

He hurried to her side and knelt beside her. "Please don't be scared of me. I'm not going to hurt you. My wife and I would like for you to come home with us and be our daughter," he said softly.

"No, I want my mommy and daddy," she replied tearfully.

He took hold of her hand. "I'm afraid that isn't possible. I'm sorry, but they're dead."

"I want to be dead too," she cried.

"No, you don't. You have your whole life ahead of you," he said, rubbing his hand up and down her back as he tried to comfort her.

"Where are my sisters? Why can't I be with them?"

Terrance had to make a quick decision. Should he tell the child the truth or should he lie to her about the rest of her family? If she thought her family was gone, would she accept being adopted easier? He thought she would. "I'm sorry, but they're gone too." So, another lie was told to one of the sisters. Lindsay didn't even think to question him about his lie, as she began sobbing and he gently put his arm around her. "Please say you will come home with me. My wife and I can't have children and we so much want a little girl to love."

"What will happen to be me if I don't go with you?"

"You'll be put into a foster home."

"Is that a bad place?" she asked, staring into the man's eyes.

"We do the best we can to ensure every child has a good home, but sometimes the foster home is overcrowded, and the child suffers because there aren't adequate beds or sufficient food to go around. If you come to live with us, you'll have your own room, and won't ever go hungry."

"I guess I'll come live with you," she replied miserably, her heart aching. She was too young to realize she had been lied to, but even if she had known the truth, at her age, it really wouldn't have changed her destiny.

"Thank you. Let's go get your suitcase and I'll take you to my home to meet my wife."

Thirty minutes later, Lindsay was being introduced to Margie Thurn and her new home, and as the years passed, Lindsay slowly forgot about her old family and accepted the new family as her own.

* * *

LESLEY

Lesley opened her eyes, her throat hurt, but she had been told that it would be sore for a few days. She turned her head and when she saw her mother, she smiled. When she noticed her mother's heart-wrenching expression on her face, her smile disappeared. "Mommy, what's wrong?"

Pam took hold of Lesley's hand. "I have some bad news to tell you."

Lesley's eyes watered up. "Am I dying?" she asked, her lip trembling.

Pam forced a smile. "No sweetheart," she said, stroking her daughter's forehead. "I'm afraid it's just you and me now. Your father and sisters are gone."

"Where did they go?" Lesley couldn't understand why her family left without her.

Pam took a deep breath before responding. "They're all dead."

"Dead!" she shrieked, then regretted it as pain ran through her throat.

"I've moved us to a two-bedroom apartment across town and you'll be going to a different school. Won't that be exciting?" she asked animatedly.

"I don't want to go to another school," she said, pouting as she looked at her mother.

"I don't care what you want," her mother screamed.

Lesley wasn't used to her mother yelling at her and began to cry.

Pam pulled her daughter into her arms. "I'm sorry sweetheart. Mommy didn't mean to yell at you. Things are going to be difficult for us for a while. We'll just have to help each other to get use to this new life."

"Okay, Mommy."

"That's my girl," she replied, relieved that Lesley accepted her lie so easily.

Two days later Lesley came home to their new apartment. Her mother took her to her new room, and she saw all her toys were there. The room looked almost the same as it had at her old home, except this one didn't have her sister or her sister's bed in it.

"Why don't you rest until lunch? If you need me, I'll be in my bedroom working on the computer. After lunch, I have some items I need to throw away."

"I don't think I could go to sleep, my throat hurts too badly," she whined.

"I'll get you your pain pills."

Pam left the room, then returned with a glass of water and two pain pills. She gave them to Lesley and tucked her into bed. After her mother left, Lesley got out of bed to investigate her new home without her mother watching over her. While she was in the kitchen, she saw several boxes stacked against the wall. Curious to what could be in them, she went to the first box and opened it. Right on top were some pictures of her and her sisters, including her favorite picture of her and Lindsay together.

Lesley grabbed several of the pictures, closed the box, and then hurried back to her room, quickly closing her door. She ran to the bed, but before she could reach it, she tripped and the pictures flew into the air, landing on top of her pink bedspread.

When she looked down at the pictures, she let out a cry, as her favorite picture wasn't among them, and she assumed must have dropped it on the way to her room. She was about to go back to look for it, but when she heard her mother outside her room, she quickly gathered the pictures and hid them under her bed. Then she jumped onto the bed, quickly laying down, and tightly closing her eyes.

As the pain pill began to take effect, Lesley relaxed and soon was asleep. When she woke, she ran to find the picture she'd lost, but there wasn't any sign of it. Lesley figured her mother must have found it and thrown it away.

CHAPTER ONE
MARCH 2007

As Mariah Clemmens glanced down at her only family picture, she had of her and her sisters, her tears threaten to fall. Every time she looked at the picture, it made her wish her childhood had been different. She had learned to love her adopted parents and the memory of that day her life had changed so drastically had faded somewhat over the past twenty years, but the hurt from the loss of her family was still there in her heart.

If it hadn't been for Evan Clemmens, the man who was her husband, her heart would still be empty. Mariah Faber had been twenty-three when she was hired at Clemmens' Manufacturing, a company ran by three brothers, to be Chandler Clemmens' assistant.

Evan the oldest brother, was the company's President, Chandler was the Vice President of the company, and Casey, the youngest brother, who had founded the company, kept the company running smoothly.

When she met Evan, sexual sparks had flown between the two of them, and six months later, they were married. A year after they were married, her adoptive parents were killed in a freak airplane accident, and now Evan and his family were the only family she had left. Recently she and Evan had a terrible argument, just minutes before he was to leave town on a business trip. Her feelings had been hurt by his comment regarding them adopting his nephew, but she knew deep down he hadn't meant the words to sound the way they had.

Between thinking of her sisters and her fight with her husband, she gave up trying to prevent the tears and let them fall. She grabbed the picture, brought it up against her chest, and she began to sob.

The television was on for noise, and when the news program penetrated her brain, she looked over at it. The story was regarding two brothers, who after a ten years separation had found each other. A smile came across her face, one similar to the sun coming out on a rainy day, as the thought of searching for her sisters formed in her head. She would start looking for them immediately, then she wiped her tears away and smiled as she sat down at the computer to begin her search.

* * *

Evan Clemmens knew he'd had too much to drink, but he didn't care, he wasn't going anywhere tonight. He was missing his wife and had hoped the drinking would help him forget her. They'd had a horrific fight about Austin, his infant nephew, regarding getting custody of him.

Mariah wanted to take on the responsibility of raising the baby after the death of Evan's half-sister and her husband, but he told her he wasn't ready to be anyone's father, and especially didn't want to raise someone else's child. It wasn't until the words were out of his mouth that he realized what he'd said, knowing his words had hurt his wife regarding adopting Austin.

After his comment to her, they both had said terrible things to each other, but his words to her had been the worst. He loved his wife and wouldn't ever purposely do anything to distress her, but he had. Mariah still had scars from her childhood and his words had hit a raw nerve, and he felt dreadful for hurting her feelings. Not only had he hurt the woman he loved, he wasn't even sure if he had a marriage to go home to or not, for she had shouted she wanted a divorce before he had a chance to apologize.

He glanced up from his drink when he noticed a woman out of the corner of his eye had sat down next to him. He turned to look at her, and in his drunken state, he thought she was Mariah, as she looked like his wife. He took in a deep breath, the aroma of her perfume was the same one she always wore, the one her birth mother had worn it, as it one of the few things Mariah did remember from her childhood.

What he couldn't understand was why she looked younger than the last time he'd seen her, then he figured his drinking must have fuddled his mind. He moved closer to her when he heard a familiar voice ordered a drink. "Sweetheart, please forgive me," he said with a slur.

Whitney turned to the man next to her. "Sir, I don't know you. I believe you have me confused with someone else." She picked up her drink the bartender sat down in front of her and started to leave, then she gazed over at the man, noticing his forlorn expression, she sighed. Whitney saw the man was drunk and probably could use a friend. She sat back down on the barstool as what could it hurt to listen to this man's story. "Do you want to talk about it?"

"Mariah, I was wrong."

"Sir, I'm not Mariah," she said, thinking that the woman's name sounded familiar to her.

"Since when? I don't understand. Why did you change it?" he asked, his voice rising in his anger.

"I'm not Mariah," she repeated. "My name is Whitney O'Rourke," she told him, taking in a deep breath, smelling his aftershave, which was too strong for her taste. "Maybe I should leave since I seem to be upsetting you."

His hand reached out and tightly gasped her wrist. "No, you aren't upsetting me."

"Is Mariah your wife?"

"She was," he replied sadly, then looked away from her, but didn't continue speaking.

"You want to tell me about her."

"I don't know where to start," he mumbled, thinking of how much he loved Mariah.

"Start at the beginning," Whitney said, prepared to listen to the man talk about his wife, whom she assumed had recently passed away.

"I'm Evan Clemmens," he said, then started his story of his and his wife's meeting.

The love he had for his wife brought tears to Whitney's eyes. He had the kind of marriage she had always wanted for herself, the kind of marriage that lasted for a lifetime. It broke Whitney's heart to listen to the man talk about the woman he'd loved. She wasn't sure how long his wife had been dead, but by the way, he was talking, it hadn't been too long.

The drinking continued as the man poured out his love for his wife to her. When the night came to an end, neither of them remembering how it had concluded.

* * *

Mariah sat looking out the window in the quiet, empty house. Why had she fought with Evan? They weren't one of those couples who were always arguing over one silly thing or another. They had been married for five years and this had been their first fight. The argument had ended with her informing him she wanted him out of her life and was going to file for divorce while he was gone on his trip.

Now she was sorry for all her angry words. She wanted to have a child to love, but what good would it be if Evan wasn't in her and the baby's life? She had to talk to him so they could straighten out this problem, but when she called his cell phone, no one answered. When his voice mail came on, she hung up instead of leaving him a message, deciding she would keep trying to get him until he answered the phone himself. Sometime after midnight, she fell asleep on the couch with her hand still on the phone.

* * *

Whitney opened her eyes, she winced as the daylight filtering into the room caused a pain to shoot through her head. She instantly knew she shouldn't have drunk as much as she had last night. She wasn't much of a drinker and hadn't realized how strong the drinks were until it was too late. She felt a movement next to her, which scared her, causing her to come instantly alert.

As her heart pounded furiously in her chest, she quickly turned her head to see who was with her. When she spied the man from last night next to her, she let out a loud swear word. He stirred and she promptly covered her mouth with her hands as tears sprung in her eyes.

She glanced around and when she realized she wasn't in her room, she assumed she was in his. She quietly crept out of the man's bed, gasping loudly when she gazed her naked body in the mirror above the dresser.

Her eyes immediately jerked to the bed, hoping she hadn't wakened him by her loud intake of breath. The last thing she wanted was for him to open his eyes and discover her in his room, especially when she didn't have a snitch of clothing on. She snatched up her clothes, then swiftly moved to the bathroom so she could get dressed in private. Once she had her clothes on, she slowly opened the door, and stepped back into the room.

She looked over at the dresser and saw the man's billfold, then quickly glanced over at the sleeping man. By the sound of his snoring, she knew he was still sleeping. Soundlessly she moved to the dresser, picked up the wallet, and quickly opened it. When she saw his business card, she pulled it out. His name was Evan Clemmens and he lived in Kansas City, Missouri, the same as she did. How odd it was for two strangers to meet in a city several miles from their home and end up living just a few miles from each other. What an unlikely occurrence!

At least now, she had more than a name to go with the man. She sat the billfold back on the dresser, but when she went to put the card in her pants pocket, it dropped to the floor. When she looked down at it, she spied a penciled heart on the back of the card. Surprised at the sight of the man and his wife's name in the middle of the heart, tears abruptly came to her eyes as she thought of this man's love for his wife. How she wished she could find a man who would love her as much as this man loved his wife. She bent down to picked up the card and hurriedly put it in her pocket.

She gazed around the room for any sign she'd been there, but there wasn't anything to indicate she had. She couldn't put her finger on it, but something didn't seem quite right to her, something that screamed for her attention. Before she could figure out what it could be, the man turned over in his sleep, causing her to jump and tightly grasped her purse in her fist. Her eyes never leaving the man on the bed, she slowly opened the door and silently let herself out, then softly pulled closed the door behind her.

When his door latched closed, she hurried to her room. Once there, she swiftly undressed, letting the clothes drop to the floor. When she was naked, she stepped into the bathroom and started the shower, turning the knobs to the hottest temperature setting she could possibly stand. She stepped in, letting the scalding water flow over her as she viciously scrubbed her body, especially between her legs. As she cleaned her body of any signs of last night activity, she began to cry.

Her tears continued as she scoured her head with shampoo, wanting the scent of that man off her, as it was all she could smell since she woke up. She shook her head at the thought of having sex with a total stranger, speculating at all the things she had done with him in that bed.

She wasn't the type of woman to go to a man's room and had sex with him. In fact, she had only been with one other man in her young life. She could blame the drinking, but it was more than that, she'd been lonely and had wanted someone to want her. When the tears finally stopped, she turned off the water and grabbed a towel to rub her body dry. As she stepped out of the tub, a frightening thought entered her head as she suddenly realized what had been bothering her concerning the room she'd just left. Birth control! She didn't remember seeing any condom wrappers lying around the room.

Her mother had drilled into her to be prepared for sex, and she made sure to carried condoms with her just in case the opportunity arose. She ran out of the bathroom, grabbed her purse, and threw it open. She dumped out the contents of her purse onto the bed and quickly counted the little packages.

Damn! Every one of them was there. If they had used any sort of protection, the man would have provided it, but if they had, where had the condom wrapper been left? She hadn't seen any in his bathroom's trashcan, but maybe he'd thrown it into the trash container beside the bed. She looked up and glanced into the mirror, shocked to see the frightened naked woman staring back at her. She could only hope the man had thought clearly enough at the time to use a condom.

* * *

Evan opened his eyes when he heard a noise and his dazed sleepy mind wondered what it could have been. He sat up quickly, then just as fast, dropped his head back to the pillow, as the pain pounding in his brain told him he had drunk too much last night. He closed his eyes and fell back to sleep for another hour. When he woke, he laid there trying to focus his mind, and realized the room smelled of Mariah's perfume. How could that be possible? Mariah was hundreds of miles away from him and probably still mad at him. As the fog seemed to clear in his head, the aroma made him think of the young woman he'd talked to at the bar last night.

Part of his mind remembered naked limbs and hot lovemaking. Did they have sex? No! He wouldn't have done that, as he was a happily married man. Well, he had been happily married until their fight. He shook his head as if to empty his mind of his sexual thoughts, but instantly regretted it. His cell phone on the dresser rang, causing him to jump; he stood, wobbled to the phone, and grabbed it before it could ring a second time. "Hello?" he mumbled.

"Evan, I'm sorry. I didn't mean all the horrible things I said to you."

"Mariah," he croaked. "God, how I've missed you. I yearn for you so bad; I swear I can smell you in this room. I even dreamed we had sex."

"Oh, honey, that's so sweet. When are you coming home?" she asked anxiously.

Evan looked at his watch. "My plane leaves in three hours."

"I'll be waiting for you," she purred.

He looked up and glanced at his face in the mirror. He grimaced, as he looked awful this morning. "You want me to come home?"

"Yes. We'll work through this."

"Mariah, I've been thinking," he started slowly.

"Don't say it. Don't tell me you're leaving me," she cried. "I promise I won't talk about us adopting Austin again."

"No, I wasn't going to say that. I was going to say you were right. It is time for us to start our family. If you want to adopt Austin, we will. I'll talk to Casey as soon as I get home."

"Evan, what if Casey doesn't want to give him up." She dreaded asking her brother-in-law for the child, but

Casey was a single man, and the child needed to have a mother and a father. If she and Evan took Austin, at least he would still be with family.

"If he won't, we'll just have to start on a baby of our own." He smiled at the thought of getting Mariah pregnant with his child.

"It might take several tries," she teased.

Evan laughed. "We'll keep at it until we get the job done right."

"Evan, thank you."

"It will be my pleasure," he said, then chuckled.

"I love you, Evan."

"I love you, Mariah. I'll call you when we've landed so you know when to expect me."

"I'll be waiting for your call. Bye."

"Bye." Evan disconnected the phone and put it back on the dresser. He knew he had to get busy if he wanted to be at the airport in time for his flight. He shaved, took a quick shower, and then rushed around his room packing his bag. He hailed a cab and arrived at the airport with plenty of time to spare.

He had been one of the first passengers to board, and when he arrived at his seat, he moved towards the window and sat down. He glanced outside, but the glare of the sun hurt his head so badly that he quickly lowered the blind and turned his head away. As he waited for take-off, he watched the people walk down the aisle to find their seats, hoping no one would sit in either of the two seats in his row. All he wanted was quiet trip home so he could recover from his hangover; maybe even take a small nap before seeing his wife. He closed his eyes against the pain of a headache that had started just behind his eyes, but they flew open when he felt something hit his arm. He turned to see what had hit him and saw a young woman had sat down in the aisle seat and saw her coat had hit his arm as she laid it in the seat between them.

"I'm sorry," she said, smiling at him.

"That's okay." He glanced away, and then promptly jerked his head around to look at the woman again. How could this be possible? The young woman looked like Mariah too, but she even looked younger than the woman he met last night. He tried to think of the woman's name from the bar, but he couldn't remember. Had she even told it to him? He wondered what had happened to her. How late was it when he had returned to his room? He really must be loaded last night, that or he was losing his mind because he couldn't even recall walking back to his hotel room. Maybe the fight with Mariah had upset him more than he originally thought.

"Excuse me sir, but is there a reason why you keep staring at me like you've seen a ghost?"

"I'm sorry, I didn't mean to stare. It's just that you look like my wife, only younger," he said, as he continued to stare at her, knowing that Mariah would want to meet this woman.

Lindsay thought this was the strangest pick up line she'd ever heard. "I don't know whether to take that as a complement or an insult," she replied curtly.

"It wasn't meant to be either; I was just stating a fact. I'm Evan Clemmens," he said, putting his hand out to her.

"It's nice to meet you," Lindsay replied coolly, as she didn't feel like being picked up by a married man. She turned away from him and opened the book in her lap.

He knew better get her name and at least find out where she lived so he could tell Mariah about her. "And you are?"

"I'm Miss Haggard," she said hesitantly, not really wanting to engage him in a conversation.

"Where are you from?" Evan asked her.

Lindsay didn't turn to look at him. "I live in Kansas City, Missouri."

"Great, we do too. I really would love my wife to meet you. Soon in fact," he told her excitedly.

She turned towards him, confusion in her eyes. "You would? Why?" What was with this guy? Was he trying to pick her up or not? She certainly wasn't into a sexually threesome.

"I wasn't kidding when I said you looked like my wife, so much so that you two could be sisters. You see, her family was torn apart when she was a young girl and hasn't seen her sisters since she was a young girl." Evan wondered if he had told the woman from last night that, but he'd been too drunk to remember much of their conversation.

His words hit Lindsay with a strange feeling, but she couldn't figure out what it could be.

"Let me give you my card." Evan got his wallet out and opened it to get the business card he always had on him, but it was gone. That was strange. Where could it have gone? He didn't remember giving it to anyone, then he thought back to the woman at the bar. Maybe he had talked to her about how much she looked like Mariah and given her his card after all. "Sorry, I seem to have given it away. Do you have something I could write on?"

"Sir, I really don't think I need to meet your wife. I'm sorry, but I can't be her sister."

"Please," he begged.

"I'm not her sister." Lindsay smiled at the man. "I'm an only child."

"Maybe that isn't true. Maybe you were adopted and just forgotten about it. Do you look like anyone in your family?" he asked, hoping she would say she didn't.

Lindsay was shock by his statement. Maybe this man was right, for as long as she could remember, she'd always wondered why she didn't look like either of her parents. Why didn't her parents have any pictures of her as a baby or as a toddler? The first pictures they had of her were when she was about five. She asked her mother about it once and she told Lindsay there had been a fire and all her baby pictures had been lost, but she hadn't believed her. "Okay, we'll exchange names and phone numbers."

He smiled at her. "I can't wait to tell Mariah I've met someone who could be her sister."

Lindsay's face quickly turned pale, as somewhere in the back of her mind, his wife's name rang a bell. Why would the woman's name seem so familiar to her? Could his wife be her sister? Why had she always felt as if a vital part of her was missing? Could it be she wasn't who she thought she was? Maybe Mariah was the part that had been missing.

"Are you okay?" He reached out and touched her arm.

Lindsay turned to stare at the man. "For some reason I know that name, but I don't know why. It isn't one of those names you hear every day."

Evan beamed at her. "Maybe it's because she *is* your sister."

"If that's true, then that means my parents have lied to me all my life," she cried.

He squeezed her arm. "Don't think of it that way. If you are her sister, your parents probably didn't talk about the adoption because at the time you were old enough to remember it. They didn't want to remind you of it, so they never talked about it. Then as time passed you forgot about your old family and before you knew it, you didn't have any memories of not being their child," he said, trying to give her some sort of comfort.

She nodded. "I guess that could've happened. How old is your wife?"

"She's twenty-nine now. She was nine when her parents died, and she was put into a foster home. How old are you?"

"I'm twenty-five." Her face cringed at the sound of a crying baby somewhere behind them, as the sound had caused her breasts to start leaking milk as soon as she heard the baby's first cry. She tried to ignore it as she tried to pay attention to what the man was saying to her. Surely, the mother of the child would do something soon to quiet the baby.

"If you are her sister, then you're one of the twins," he said, beaming at her.

Lindsay's attention quickly returned to him and her eyes began to water. "Twins? If I am your wife's sister, then I have a twin?" She wiped the tear away. That would explain why she had the sensation that a part of herself was absent in her life. "What kind of twin?" she asked, squeezing hard on his arm.

"An identical twin sister."

"Do you really think I'm Mariah's sister?" she asked emotionally, then she held her breath, waiting for his response.

He grinned and nodded. "What is your first name?"

"It's Lindsay."

Evan smiled at her. "Your name is the same as Mariah's sister. If you are her sister, your twin sister's name is Lesley, and you have a sister two years older named Whitney. You are the first one to be found, as Mariah hasn't had any luck finding the others yet. All she has from her childhood is a picture of the four of you before their parents' death."

"Her sisters' names seem familiar too. Do you have a picture of your wife?"

"No, but she is going to pick me up at the airport, so you can meet her then." He watched as she started to squirm in her seat. "Is something wrong? Are you feeling sick?" he asked with concern.

The baby's cry became louder. "I can't bear to hear a baby cry like that. Excuse me, but I have to take care of this matter."

CHAPTER TWO

Lindsay stood up to look behind her and four seats back, she saw a man trying to quiet an upset infant. She quickly hurried down the aisle and stopped in front of the man with the crying infant. "Is there something I can do to help?" she inquired, looking down at the handsome, but frustrated man. In his arms, he was holding a crying baby approximately two months old, who was refusing to take hold of the nipple of the bottle in front of him.

Casey Pennay looked up at her and his jaw dropped, surprised to see a woman who reminded him of his oldest brother's wife standing beside him. But what shocked him the most about her was his body's instantly response to her beauty. He was confused by his body's reaction, since he'd never reacted this way towards Mariah, as he thought of her as a sister.

First, his heart began hammering in his chest; his mouth became dry, as if he had a bunch of cotton balls in it, and a hard arousal pushing on his pants zipper. Luckily for him, Austin's blanket covered that part of his body. He figured she was there to complain about the baby's crying, and he forced himself to swallow. "Not unless you have some other way to feed him other than this bottle," Casey replied coldly.

"Excuse me?" Lindsay didn't understand why his anger was directed at her.

"Austin won't take the bottle. My sister was nursing him."

"Where's your sister now?" she inquired, looking around the plane to find the child's mother.

"My sister, Alexandra and her husband, Clayton, were killed recently. Clayton's sister had been taking care of the baby until I could arrive to get him. She had a year-old daughter who she had been nursing, so she was able to feed him, but she couldn't keep Austin. I was hoping if he was hungry enough, he would take the bottle, but he proved me wrong." He was frustrated at the situation, knowing the people around him were tired of listening to Austin's crying.

"I'm so sorry for your lost." Lindsay understood his sorrow of losing his sister and her husband. Lindsay's husband, Bryon, had been dead for almost two years now and she still hurt from the lost. "May I try to feed him?"

"You believe you can get him to take the bottle when I couldn't?" he shouted angrily at her.

She smiled at him. "No, I was going to nurse him," she responded pleasantly.

"What? Is this some kind of sick joke? You think my situation is funny?" he asked in a huff.

"No, of course not. I'm only trying to help. I'm Lindsay Haggard. May I sit?" she asked, pointing to the empty seat by the window.

"Yes," he replied, watching the young woman closely. For some reason her name seemed familiar, but he knew he hadn't ever met her before, as he would've remembered if he had. "I'm Casey Pennay, and this is Austin Wilson."

Lindsay processed slowly passed him and the second seat, which had the infant's car seat sitting in it. She sat down in the seat next to the window and put her purse on the floor. "Could I have the baby?" The man frowned at her. "Please." She could tell the man was unsure of her and her offer to help.

Casey stood and handed her the crying infant as she reached out to take him. The sensation of the infant in her arms was almost too much for her and her heart began thumping in her chest and her breasts aching to feel the baby's mouth on her nipple. How she'd missed nursing and taking care of a little one. When Casey continued to stand there watching her, she grinned at him. "I promise I won't steal him."

His eyes had been on her breasts instead of listening to what she had been saying. "What?" His eyes jerked to her face in time to see her blush. "I'm sorry for staring," he muttered, feeling like an idiot at getting caught staring at her breasts like a teenager.

She didn't say anything to him regarding where his eyes had been. "You can sit back down; I'm not going anywhere with him."

"Oh." Casey sat down but didn't remove his eyes from her.

Lindsay covered herself with his blanket before positioning the baby in her arms. She reached under her blouse to unhook her nursing bra, and then put the baby to her breast. He started suckling as soon as his mouth touched her nipple. Lindsay smiled in relief, even though she felt the other breast leaking, but with any luck, the breast pad in her bra would soak up the excess before it could leak out onto her blouse. She would wait to change the pad until after she was done feeding the baby.

When the cabin became quiet other than the sound of the blissfully nursing baby, the people around them applauded and the man's face turned red from the embarrassment.

How could she nurse Austin? He didn't understand how this was possible. "How can you nurse him? I didn't think you could do that unless you had a baby." His eyes watched her closely.

"I have a fifteen-month-old daughter who I've just weaned to a cup, but my milk hasn't had time to dry up yet. Didn't matter if it was breast milk or not, she still wouldn't take a bottle either."

"Where's your daughter? Is she up front with your husband?"

"I'm returning home without her. I left her with my in-laws for a week's visit. Now that she is drinking from a cup, I can leave her with them." She didn't explain about Bryon because sometimes it made people uncomfortable when they find out her husband was dead. "Once you get home, you'll have to check into finding someone who can be his wet nurse."

"There are people are willing to do that?" He was shocked at her comment.

"Check with an organization called La Leche League. Some infants are allergic to all types of formula, and the group help get breast milk to babies whose mothers can't nurse for one reason or another. Maybe they'll know someone who could help you. Do you have any other family that will be able to assist you with the baby?"

"Yes, I have three brothers and a sister-in-law. My oldest brother's wife wants to adopt Austin, but my brother doesn't want to raise someone else's child. My other two brothers aren't married and can't take him. My sister and I were very close, and I feel it is my responsibility to take care of him."

"I can understand that. I assume there's no wife at home?" she asked, even though she hadn't seen a wedding ring.

"No," he replied, wishing this woman could be his wife, but knew that wasn't possible.

"Who is going to take care of him while you're working?"

"I don't know. I haven't had the opportunity to check into it," he replied sadly.

She moved the baby to her other breast to finish feeding him, then looked up at the man. When she noticed him intensely staring at her breast again and she loudly cleared her throat.

His eyes jerked upward. "Sorry," he replied, his cheeks turning red.

She didn't respond. She hadn't been attracted to a man for a long time, but for some reason his gaze had excited her. She would have liked to have stayed and talked to him, but it was time to get back to her seat and the man who may be her sister's husband. When the baby fell asleep, she pulled him away from her and quickly covered herself. Then she put him to her shoulder and began patting his back. After the soft burp, she put him in his car seat, and sat back down. "It can all be overwhelming." She picked up her purse, opened it, and pulled out a business card. "If for some reason you should need to talk or ask any questions, please don't hesitate to call me." She reached over and gave him her card. "I work from my home, so don't be afraid to call any time, day, or night," she said pleasantly, wishing she could tell him how he made her feel.

"Lindsay Haggard, Novelist," he read. "I knew your name seemed familiar, now I know why. I saw some of your books at my sister's house when I packed up her belongings. I didn't notice at the time, but what kind of novels do you write?"

"Romance," she told him, fighting to prevent from blushing, but wasn't successful. For some reason talking to this man on the subject of romance had embarrassed her. Maybe it was because she was attracted to him.

Casey noticed her blush and wondered what had caused it. Was she attracted to him too? "Won't your husband mind a strange man calling you in the middle of the night?"

"No," she replied, feeling bad for not telling him about Bryon.

"Do you mind if I talk to him to make sure it's okay with him?" The last thing he wanted was to cause trouble for this woman since she'd save the day for him.

Lindsay knew she had to tell him the truth. "Mr. Pennay, I have to be honest with you concerning my husband."

Casey's first thought was she was an unwed mother and she had had her baby without the benefit of having a husband, he was instantly embarrassed for mentioning he wanted to talk to her husband. "Don't worry about it," he said, looking away from her.

"No, I want to tell you. Bryon died shortly after I found out I was expecting Nicole."

He quickly turned to look at her. "I'm so sorry," he said, then a puzzled look appeared on his face. "I don't understand. Why didn't you say so in the first place?"

She gave him a weak smile. "Sometimes when people find out my husband died while I was pregnant, they feel uncomfortable. With strangers who I'll most likely never see again, I usually don't mention he's dead. I'm still wearing my wedding ring so when people see it, they just assume I have a husband in my life."

"I see." A quick thought came to him regarding Austin. "You said you work from home."

Her eyes were observing him closely, and when he seemed engrossed with a thought, she sensed he had come up with some sort of strategy. "That's right," she replied slowly, nervous about his expression.

He beamed at her. "Would you be able to take Austin?"

"What?" she squawked, shocked by his question. This wasn't at all what she thought he was thinking. "I'm not going to take your nephew. He should be with family, not some stranger."

He put his hands up to calm her. "I don't mean for good. Just until I can find someone else to help me with him."

"Mr. Pennay . . . ," she started, but he interrupted.

"Please call me Casey," he told her.

"I know you want what's best for your nephew, but I can't help you. I have a book deadline to meet and don't have much time to complete my book. That's why Nicole is with her grandparents, so I can work without any interruptions. I'm sorry, but I can't take care of him even if I wanted to."

"I know I don't have a right to ask you, but I'm begging you. I'll come to your place, I'll do the housework, cook your dinner, and do your laundry. Anything! Please," he begged, his hand reached out and clutched her hand. "I'm desperate."

His sad eyes are what did her in, as she just didn't have the heart to tell him no again. "How soon do you have to return to work?"

His face lit up with a sexy grin as he lifted her hand and kissed it. "Thank you."

She quickly pulled her hand away from his. "I haven't said I'll watch him yet."

He continued to smile at her. "I'm in business with brothers, one is the President, and the other is the Vice President. My job is to keep the company running smoothly, which isn't hard to do, so I can come and go as I please."

"If we set up some sort of arrangement, we might be able to make this work," she told him, trying to think what he could do to help her with her book.

"What did you have in mind?" he inquired, trying not to let her know that his mind was in the gutter. For he was thinking about taking her to bed, so she could take care of his other needs as well as taking care of Justin.

"Do you know anything about of the Internet?" she asked, realizing what it was that he could do to help.

His mind snapped back to the real world. "Enough to work my way around on it. Why do you ask?"

"Since my husband's death, I've been having trouble writing. It's as if I have a mental block or something. In my case, I think it is more of an emotion block. If you could help me with my research so I can finish my book before the deadline, I'll help you with Austin."

An ornery thought entered his head as he again thought of sex with her. "Should we move in together?" he asked, laughing when he saw her scandalized expression. "I take that as a no."

"I probably should have Austin with me twenty-four seven, but I don't think you and I will have to be together that much."

"It would make things easier on all of us if we lived in the same house," he verbalized softly, still thinking about having her in his bed.

"You mean it will be less trouble for you," she said, with hostility.

"All right, it will make things easier for me. Someday I'm going to have full charge of Austin. I have to be ready, so I know what to do once it's just me and him."

Lindsay nodded. "I'm sorry for my comment. I hadn't thought of that, but you're right." She looked away and then looked back at him. "It probably would make more sense if I moved in with you."

"Why do you say that?" he asked, not caring where they lived, but the thought of them in bed together set him aflame.

"Your place is going to be his home. It's best to have him settled in one place. We haven't any idea how long our association is going to be, but I'd say he probably could be weaned to a cup somewhere around nine months, six months at the earliest, and a year at the longest."

"What about your daughter? How is she going to take moving into my home?"

"As long as she's with me, I'm sure she'll be fine."

The plane's captain announced they would be landing at Kansas City in ten minutes.

"I need to get back to my seat, I'm sure your nephew should be fine for a couple of hours. The man I was sitting next to wants me to meet his wife, so I don't want to lose him in the bustle of leaving the plane."

Casey watched as Lindsay stood, but prevented her from passing him. "Why does he want you to meet his wife?"

"Not that it is any of your business, but he thinks I maybe one of his wife's sisters."

"That's a new one," he replied sarcastically, letting out a loud snort.

Lindsay looked at him, surprised by his comment. "What is that supposed to mean?"

"You're a beautiful woman. I'm sure a man would try to find any way he could to be able to get involved with you."

"He said I looked like his wife, not that he wanted to take me to bed."

"And you believed him? I think you look enough like my sister-in-law to be related to her too, but you didn't hear me feeding you such a line."

She sat back down in the seat and looked at him with bewilderment. "What is your sister-in-law's name?" she asked, thinking that maybe she could be one of her other sisters.

"Mariah Clemmens."

Lindsay laughed. "I don't believe this."

"What's so funny?" His facial features scrunched up, indicating he didn't think anything concerning their conversation humorous.

"What is your brother's name?" she asked with a slight smile.

"Which brother's name do you want?"

"The brother who's married to the woman who looks like me," she answered with a grin.

"His name is Evan Clemmens, but I don't why you want to know that."

She was confused by the different last names. "If he's your brother, why don't you two have the same last name?"

"My sister and I had a different father than our two brothers."

"Would you believe he's the man I was talking about?"

"What?"

"He's sitting just a few rows ahead of us?"

"Evan is on this plane? I don't believe it."

"If the man I was sitting next to earlier was truthful regarding his name, he is."

The flight attendant announced everyone needed to return to his or her seats and buckle their seatbelts.

"I need to be back to my seat."

"I need you for Austin." Casey grasped her hand. "I don't want to lose sight of you once we land."

"You have my card in case we get separated and my cell number is on it. I'll turn on my phone as soon as we land."

"Fine," he said grumpily, unhappy about her leaving him alone with Austin.

As she passed by him, she smiled at him, then stepped out into the aisle. He watched as she turned and started down the aisle. His emotions were jumbled as she disappeared from his sight, as he hadn't ever had a woman affect him quite like this before. What did it all mean? Was this what Mariah had meant when she talked about love at first sight? Could he be falling in love with Lindsay? Impossible! Maybe they could get to know each other, then maybe it would lead somewhere for them, but then maybe he just needed to get laid.

When Lindsay returned to her original seat, Evan reached over and seized a tight hold of her hand. "I was afraid you weren't going to return."

She smiled at him. "I was just a few seats behind you. There aren't too many places I could have gone to on this plane."

"I know, but still I want you to meet my wife."

"Do you have a brother named Casey?"

Evan looked at her, confused as to where this question had come from. He couldn't figure out how this woman could know anything regarding his brother. "Yes," he replied slowly, "why do you ask?"

"Austin was the infant you heard crying earlier." Lindsay grinned at him. "He and Austin are sitting behind us."

Evan stood up and looked behind him. Sure enough, he saw Casey looking back at him. He smiled and waved at him, then he sat back down. "I didn't know he was returning this soon," he said, baffled to why Casey was on this flight. "Why was the baby crying? Is he sick or something?" He wouldn't want to take on the responsibility of caring for a sick child, no matter how much Mariah wanted him.

"No, just hungry."

"Didn't Casey have a bottle for him?"

"He did, but Austin is a breastfed baby, who hadn't ever had a bottle before and refused to take it. Some babies are like that, while other breastfed babies don't mind taking a bottle occasionally."

"Did Casey inform you my wife wanted to adopt Austin?"

"Yes, he did," she said, but didn't elaborate, thinking she would let him tell her the rest if he wanted her to know.

"Did he also tell you that I said that I didn't want him?" he asked, even though he figured Casey had told her.

She nodded. "Yes, he did."

"Mariah and I've talked recently. If Casey will let us, we want to adopt Austin."

"You shouldn't be telling me this. You need to talk to your brother."

"I will as soon as I can."

The plane landed, taxied down the landing strip, then finally stopped next to the terminal. As soon as the flight attendant announced they could start disembarking, people stood and started taking their carry-on luggage down from the overhead compartments. Lindsay waited until Casey came up the aisle with Austin in his carrier before she stepped out into the aisle in front of him, with Evan following right behind her.

Evan turned to look at his brother. "Casey, I didn't know you were on this flight. I thought you would still be in Oklahoma." His eyes showed his bafflement.

"I finished my business faster than I thought I would," he replied melancholy.

"What about the funeral?"

"There wasn't one," he said sorrowfully.

"What?" Evan was surprised to hear that. "I thought they were going to be buried in Flagstaff."

"Clayton's sister refused to help pay for their burial. So, I decided if we're paying the entire bill for both, I'd bring them home and buried them next to our parents."

Evan touched his brother's shoulder. "I think they would like that."

"I'm glad you think so, I wasn't sure. I wanted to call to check with all of you, but there wasn't enough time."

"Casey, we need to talk."

Casey looked at his brother with misunderstanding. "What do we need to talk about? By your comment, I assumed it was okay with you that I was bringing Alexandra and Clayton home to be buried. So, what else do we need to talk about?"

"I meant regarding us adopting Austin."

"You told me you didn't want the baby. Your exact words were, 'I don't want to be a father, especially to someone else's kid.' Isn't that what you told me?" he asked heatedly.

Evan nodded. "I know what I said, but Mariah wants him. I love her and I want to make her happy."

"I don't know. I've just found out today Austin won't take a bottle."

"So, I'm sure he would if he was hungry enough," he replied innocently.

"What do you want to do? Starve the baby until he decides he better take a bottle or else," Casey said angrily.

"Of course not. It wouldn't take him long before he would take the nourishment from a bottle."

Casey shook his head at his brother's words. "Did you hear him screaming earlier on the plane?"

"Yes. So?" He didn't understand what the big deal was. The baby would have to take the bottle if he was hungry enough.

"Did you enjoy listening to him scream?" he asked nastily.

"No, of course not."

"He isn't at the age you can sit down and rationally discuss the situation with him. Austin is a baby who is used to nursing and that's what he needs," he insisted.

"I don't see what the problem is."

Casey shook his head at his brother's ignorance, but then had to smile. He couldn't blame Evan for his stupidity, as he'd learned quite a bit about babies himself since taking custody of Austin. He looked in front of him to the woman who had offered to help him with the baby. If Evan and Mariah took Austin to live with them, then he wouldn't have a reason to see her and he really did want to get to know her better.

"Casey," Evan called to get his attention.

"What?" Casey's eyes returned to his brother's face.

"You didn't hear a word I said," he said, then looked where Casey had been staring and smiled. So, his baby brother was interested in Lindsay. Maybe he should tell him that she might be Mariah's sister.

"I'm sorry. What did you say?"

"I asked if you were going to tell Mariah no, because I'm not going to."

"Evan," he pleaded, hoping he could make his brother understand. "For right now I think it would be best for Austin to stay with me."

"Fine," he said hatefully, turning away from Casey.

Casey put his hand on his brother's arm. "I'm not saying you'll never have him. I just think for now Austin should live with me." When Evan didn't response to his comment, he tightened his grip on his brother's arm. "Evan, you're my brother and I love you. I wouldn't do anything to hurt you or Mariah. Alexandra was my sister; I just want to do what's best for her son."

Evan stopped and turned so quickly that Casey bumped into him, nearly dropping the baby in his carrier.

"What in the hell do you think you're doing?" he asked furiously, looking at his brother's heated expression.

"We may have had different fathers, but Alexandra was my sister too. I loved her just as much as you did," Evan said, with rage and fire in his eyes.

"I'm sorry. I shouldn't have said that the way I did. I know you, Chandler, and Morgan loved her as much as I did, but I was named Austin's guardian and I don't want to screw it up. Let's get our luggage and get out of here. We'll go to your place and have a family meeting."

Evan shook his head. "Let's not do it today. We're all tired. First, we need to bury our sister and her husband. Once that is all taken care of, we'll have a family meeting and make plans for Austin."

"Fine," Casey replied angrily, but he wasn't about to let his oldest brother make all the decisions regarding Austin.

CHAPTER THREE

They walked together side by side to the baggage claim with neither brother speaking. Once there, Casey sat Austin's carrier down to wait for his luggage, while Evan moved away from Casey to call Mariah on his cell phone. Before he finished dialing, he disconnected the call and let out a shrill whistle, causing Lindsay standing beside him to jump.

Lindsay looked over at Evan and noticed him waving at someone, and then he took off running to greet a woman. She continued to watch as he pulled the woman into his arms, giving her a hug, and then started kissing her.

She was surprised at the length of the kiss, thinking she would be embarrassed if someone kissed her like that in the middle of an airport. She wondered what he was telling her after their passionate kiss. Was he telling his wife about her? It wasn't long before she saw Mariah lean around Evan to glance at her. Lindsay just stood there staring at the woman as she started towards her. As the woman came closer to her, Lindsay couldn't believe her eyes, as the two of them did resemble each other. Could they possibly be sisters? Tears started falling down her face as Mariah stopped in front of her.

"Lindsay, is it really you?"

"I don't know if I'm the Lindsay you think I am, but I sure hope so." She reached out and put her hand on Mariah's face. "We look so much alike, it's scary. I don't want to get my hopes up and then find out we're not related."

"Do you remember anything from your childhood?"

"Your name is familiar to me, but I don't know why."

"That's all?" Mariah was disappointed by Lindsay's response, hoping this woman would have remembered her.

"Your husband mentioned Lesley and Whitney. Their names are familiar to me as well, but most of what I remember of my life is with the people who I thought were my parents."

"Can you ask them about your childhood?" she asked hopefully.

"They are both dead, and when I cleaned out the house, I didn't find anything to indicate I wasn't who I thought I was."

"You and Lesley were only five when they separated us," Mariah said, then smiled at her. "We'll have to be tested to make sure we're sisters, but I have no doubt that we're related."

"Do you know why we were torn apart the way we were?"

Before Mariah could answer, a loud burp was heard behind Lindsay. She looked around Lindsay to see Casey standing with Austin's carrier, watching the two women. "What do we have here?" She cooed as she knelt to the level of Austin in his carrier. She had tears in her eyes when she looked up at her brother-in-law. "Casey, he's beautiful."

"I think he looks like his mother," Evan said, lightly touching her shoulder. He had to tell her they weren't getting him, but the lump in his throat prevented him.

Mariah nodded. "I think you're right." She stood and looked at Casey. "Did Evan tell you that we do want him after all?"

The last thing Casey wanted was a hysterical woman in the middle of an airport, but he knew he had to tell her as soon as possible. He didn't want her to assume they were going to get him any longer than necessary. Casey sat the carrier down, stepped to his sister-in-law, and pulled her into his arms. "Mariah, I love you and I wouldn't ever do anything to hurt you."

"I hear a but here," she replied slowly, pulling out of his arms to look at him.

"But I think Austin should stay with me." Casey's heart just almost broke when Mariah's eyes filled with tears. "Just for now," he quickly added.

She looked over at her husband with a tearful expression. When Evan saw her face, he pulled her into a tight embrace. "You're single," she said, while hugging her husband. "Evan and I are married; I can quit my job to stay with him, while you'll have to hire someone to take care of him. We can make him a home," she told him tearfully.

"I'm not saying he'll never be yours. I just found out today on the flight here that Austin won't take a bottle. No matter who has him, we're going to have to hire someone to nurse him until the problem no longer exists."

"I don't understand. How are you going to feed him? I don't believe even you can do that," she said mockingly, hurt that Austin wasn't going to be hers.

Casey turned to look at Lindsay and then back at Mariah. "Lindsay can nurse him until we find someone else."

Mariah gazed at the woman who may or may not be her sister. "How can you nurse him?" Suddenly more tears welled up in her eyes, her hands reached out and clutched the younger woman's hand. "You didn't lose your baby, did you?"

Lindsay quickly squeezed Mariah's hand. "No, my daughter is alive and well. I've just weaned her to the cup and she's staying with her grandparents." She looked over at the two men who were watching them and then she leaned close to Mariah so the men couldn't hear her. "My breasts still have milk in them. That's why I can nurse your nephew," she whispered softly. She leaned back but didn't look at the men just in case they had overheard her comment.

"I see. Do you have a job that will allow you time to nurse him?"

"I work from home. He won't be any trouble at all."

Mariah was disappointed with this outcome. "I don't know what to say. I had so hope he was going to be ours."

Casey touched Mariah's arm. "He is. He's all of ours. I brought Alexandra and Clayton home to be buried next to Mom. Let's get them taken care of and Austin settled with me first, then we'll evaluate what will be best for him." He smiled weakly at her. "Okay?"

She smiled back at him. "Okay." She leaned her head against her husband and looked up at him. He winked at her, letting her know that they would start creating their own child as soon as they got home. "We need to leave as I suddenly remembered we have some important business to take care of at home."

Evan took hold of his wife's hand. "We'll be in touch."

Before Casey or Lindsay could respond, Evan grabbed his suitcase, and the couple was gone.

Lindsay was surprised by their sudden departure, but when she looked over at Casey, she noticed he didn't seem shocked by what had just happened. "What was that all about?"

"I believe they are going home to create their own little one."

"Oh!" Lindsay quickly blushed, not quite sure what else to say.

Casey laughed at her expression. "You'll get use to those two. They still act like newlyweds."

"How long have they been married?"

Casey thought for a few seconds. "I'm not for sure the exact date, but I believe it has been nearly five years. How do you want to work us living together?"

She knew he didn't mean it the way it sounded, but the thought of being naked and in this man's, bed had her heart quickly pulsating. "I need to go home to pack a few belongings for my stay at your place first. I'll need to get my laptop and some other work-related items."

"I could go with you to help."

"Thank you, but it would go faster by myself. I just have my carry-on luggage, so I can leave now and meet you at your house."

"Okay, sounds good." He quickly gave her directions to his place, then watched as she walked away, admiring the movement of her backside as she walked away. He retrieved his luggage, then went home.

While Casey waited for Lindsay to arrive, he called a funeral home to arrange Alexandra and Clayton's funeral, which he was able to schedule for Monday afternoon. He called his other two brothers, leaving each message explaining he hadn't buried Alexandra and Clayton in Oklahoma as planned, but had brought them to Kansas City to be buried next to their mother and his father, and that the funeral would be Monday.

An hour later, Lindsay pulled into his driveway, surprised to see Casey standing in the driveway. He opened the car door as soon as she turned off the motor. "Is everything okay?"

"Austin is still sleeping, so I thought I'd come out to help bring in your suitcase."

She smiled at him. "Thank you."

"I stopped and bought a baby monitor for you to use."

"How thoughtful. I'm sure I'll get plenty of use out of it," she said sincerely, giving him a sweet smile. "I love having one for Nicole, but I dropped mine recently and broke it. I hadn't had a chance to go buy a new one."

"I've thought you could sleep in the bedroom next to Austin's. I've set up the bedroom downstairs for your office."

"Does it have a phone line connection in it?"

"Both bedrooms do."

Shortly after she was settled into the bedroom she was using, she heard Austin starting to fuss and hurried into his room to tend to him. After he had on a clean diaper, she sat down in a rocking chair and made herself comfortable in it. She covered herself with the blanket just in case Casey walked in and quickly put the baby to her breast.

Casey came into the room but stopped suddenly when he spotted her with the baby and smiled as he listened to the baby nurse. "He reminds me of his father, as Clayton loved to eat."

Lindsay jumped at the unexpected sound of his voice, still not used to how her body reacted to him. After a few minutes she repositioned the baby to her other breast, trying to keep her body covered as much as possible, as the last thing she wanted was for him to see any parts of her body that he shouldn't. She nursed the baby until he fell back to sleep, then put him to her shoulder to burp him.

"Let me." Casey walked to her, taking the baby from her, making sure his hands didn't touch her breast. He burped Austin, then laid him in the crib on his back, and covered him with a blanket. He turned to look at Lindsay. "Let's go downstairs and I'll show you the room you'll be using to finish your novel."

"Okay," she uttered softly, his nearness overwhelmed her. Her attraction to him was causing her heart to pulsate rapidly and she had to close her eyes to get the image of them in bed together out of her head. She took a very deep breath, slowly letting it out before opening her eyes. When she opened them, Casey was staring at her.

"Is everything okay?"

She gave him a weak smile. "Yes, of course," she muttered, quickly turning away from him.

"You looked as if . . ." he started, but didn't finish what he was going to say, wondering if she was having the same sexual attraction to him as he was having towards her.

"I'm fine," she replied quickly. She picked up the receiver to the baby monitor as they left the baby's room, then followed him downstairs to a large bedroom.

"I stopped on the way home to buy the computer and desk for you. They were delivered just a few minutes before you arrived, but I still need to connect everything before you can use it. I plan to hook both computers to the same printer, but I'll use my computer to do your research on."

His thoughtfulness touched her. "You shouldn't have bought it. I told you I had my laptop," she told him.

They entered the bedroom and when she saw which computer he'd bought, she chuckled. "Are you trying to bribe me into staying?" As it was the exact computer, she'd wanted for herself, but hadn't wanted to spend the money to buy it yet.

"No, of course not," he denied, but the slight grin on his face, said he was lying. "I thought you could use a larger computer for your writing, as it has all the latest software already installed on it."

When she looked around the room, she saw two desks sitting back to back, with a computer screen sitting on each desk and it looked perfect. She turned to look at him. "This setup looks great," she told him, putting the baby monitor on the first desk.

"I was thinking we probably should be in the same room so that we could collaborate without having to stop and go into another room to talk, but if you want to be by yourself, I can move one of the desks to another room." He meant what he said, but he didn't want her to tell him that she wanted the room to herself.

She beamed at him. "No, this will be fine. Thank you for everything you've done. I really appreciate the gesture." She leaned over and kissed his cheek, but quickly jerked back, disturbed by the electrical current that zoomed through her when her lips touched his skin.

His eyes glanced at her mouth, then he grabbed hold of her arms, immediately pulling her to him, so her lips met his.

Just as his lips to touch hers, another electric surge shot threw her. Abruptly she pulled away and took a shaky step backwards.

His eyes flew to hers. "Oh, my!"

"I don't think us living in the same house is going to work," she said breathlessly. She took a second step backwards, her eyes filling with fright, as how could she live with this man and not go to bed with him?

Casey saw her expression and assumed he had repulsed her. "I promise I'll keep my hands to myself from now on. Please don't leave," he begged. "I really do need you."

"That's great for you, but what about me?" she asked softly, her eyes closely watching him.

He stared at her with bewilderment. "I don't understand. What do you mean? What about you?" His eyes searched her face, trying to comprehend what she was trying to tell him.

"I don't know if I can do the same," she replied honestly. "You're the first man since my husband's death that I've been attracted to." Her eyes had tears in them. "My body wants you to make love to me," she choked out her confession.

Casey was thunderstruck, as never in his life had he had a woman tell him something as intimate and erotic as what she had just said. He wasn't sure how to respond, afraid he would say the wrong thing to her. "I believe we have the beginning of something special here. It may even result in marriage or it may not. I don't want to rush you or make a mistake that may ruin what we could have together."

She smiled at his comment, touched that he'd mentioned marriage. "I appreciate your truthfulness."

"Tell me something. Are you looking for a fling or something more long term?" he asked, his eyes never leaving hers.

"I wasn't looking for anything, but especially not a fling. I'm not that kind of person. I have to be honest, I've never felt this way before," she declared, staring deeply into his eyes.

His eyebrow raised in mystification. "What about your husband?"

"There was love and affection between us, but nothing like this hot passion I felt when we kissed."

"Let me understand this," he said, stunned by her blunt comment. "You felt hot passion with just a kiss?"

She simply nodded for she couldn't say anything because of the knot in her throat.

"I don't know what to say. Before we do anything, we may regret, I must tell you that Austin is probably going to be living with me permanently."

"And I have Nicole."

He stepped closer to her. "Lindsay, will you marry me?" he asked, grabbing hold of her hands and squeezing them.

"What?" she asked, shocked by his question.

"What else can we do? We have two children to think of and neither of us wants a fling."

Tears welled up in her eyes. "Casey, don't you think we're rushing this just a bit?"

"We're going to be living in the same house until Casey takes a bottle or is weaned. With the two of us being attracted to each other and being in such close quarters together, we're bound to end up in bed together." She nodded at his comment. "Do you want more children?" His eyes searched hers, trying to anticipate her response.

"I wouldn't mind having your baby," she blurted, then a blush ran up her neck to her face.

He pulled her into his arms and passionately started kissing her. His hands moved upwards, and began unbuttoning her blouse, as his lips following his fingers. His body wanted hers so badly he was afraid his control would explode before they could get undressed.

Lindsay's mind was a complete bowl of mush, as part of her brain was telling her to make him stop, and the other part wanted to ask him to go faster. His lovemaking was breathtaking and exciting, something she hadn't had for a long time.

One minute they were standing, and the next, they were on the floor making love to each other on the plush carpet. The only problem was it was over practically before it got started. It was probably because neither of them had been with anyone for a long time, that and the heat radiating between them had been too much for them to prolong the experience.

As he laid there trying to catch his breath, he heard her crying and he tightened his embrace. "Lindsay, I'm so sorry. I don't know what came over me. Once our lips touched my body took over and my brain didn't have a chance."

"I'm not crying because I'm distraught," she whispered in his ear, thinking of how beautiful the experience had been.

"Then why are you sobbing in my arms?"

She looked deeply into his eyes, putting her hand on his face before responding. "Because it was so magnificent."

"It was that good, uh?" He smiled an ornery grin at her.

She laughed. "Yes, it was."

"So, are you ready to try it again?" he teased.

Terror filled her eyes when she realized they hadn't used any protection. "Oh, my God! Casey, we were in such a hurry we forgot to do something that's vital to our situation," she exclaimed.

"I didn't kiss your breasts?" he asked, grinning at her.

She lightly hit his arm. "No! I'm serious. We forgot to use any birth control."

"Damn!" He pulled away from her and sat up, his eyes showed he was deep in thought, his expression solemn. "We better get married as soon as possible."

She forced a shaky laugh. "Will you get serious?" She didn't appreciate his teasing, as this was a serious matter.

"I'm serious," he stated honestly. "The men in our family have always been very fertile."

She studied him for a few seconds trying to decide if he truly did want to marry her. "Even with the off chance I may have gotten pregnant just now, marriage isn't something to take lightly or jump into if you have any uncertainties."

"You think I'm taking this lightly?" he asked, torn by his conflicting emotions.

"How do I know?" she responded, hunching her shoulders. "We have known each other less than four hours. Don't you have some doubts? I know I have."

"Let's try an experiment."

She eyed him with suspicion before responding. "What kind of experiment?"

CHAPTER FOUR

He smiled a sexy grin at her. "I'll give you an amorous kiss. If neither of us feels anything, we'll forget I mentioned marriage, and we'll go on as planned. But," he started, then stopped as he looked deeply into her eyes, "if there should be fireworks again, we'll get married ASAP."

"You felt fireworks when you kissed me?" she asked, her voice cracking with emotion.

He abruptly pulled into his arms. "Oh yes," he purred into her ear, but before his lips could touch hers, a baby's cry was heard from the monitor. "I guess our experiment will have to wait."

She quickly dressed. "It's just as well," she started, thinking they would end up making love again and felt they shouldn't be doing that again until they were sure about where their relationship was going.

Her words made him angry, as he thought she hadn't felt the same fire between them that he had. "Fine," he replied angrily. "Go take care of the baby. We'll just forget about the kiss." His words sounded sharp to his own ears, then he felt bad for his harsh comment.

She laughed a bubbly giggle. "I don't think so," she said, then walked out of room to tend to the baby. As she took care of Austin's needs, she thought about her needs. The intense desire Casey caused in her was confusing. What she needed was to talk to another woman; maybe she could call Mariah and talk to her. She might turn out not to be her sister, but she was Casey's sister-in-law and she probably could give her some insight regarding this man.

Lindsay laid the baby back in the crib and covered him before leaving to find Casey. She found him in the living room watching television. He refused to look up when she entered the room, but she didn't notice as she was busy thinking what she was going to say to Mariah and hadn't been looking at him. "Casey, could I have Mariah's phone number?"

He jumped off the couch and stared angrily at her. "You going to call her and tell her all about what happen between us?" he asked her with a sneer. "I didn't think you were the type to kiss and tell." His voice was choked with his anger.

Her eyes flew to his. "I was going to talk to her about my feeling towards you, but maybe I should just repack my car and return to my home," she said sadly, her pride hurt by his cruel comment.

Casey's pride was telling him to say the hell with her; he didn't need her, as there were plenty of women in this city who would be happy to marry him. However, his heart told him to forget about his pride and stop her before she could leave, as he may never find a woman who affected him the same way she did. He was twenty-five years old and this was the first time he'd ever felt this way. He stood and walked to where she was standing rigid and proud, then he stretched out to take hold of her hand, but she moved it out of his reach.

"I'll go pack," she mumbled, tears filling her eyes.

"Lindsay, I'm sorry for my rude comment. You might find this hard to believe, but I've never been in love before. I find it all a bit scary."

She didn't know if she really believed him or not. "Are you saying you think you're in love with me?"

He took a step closer. "Yes, I am."

"Really?" She stared at him, trying to decide if he was sincere or not. "Why do you think you are?"

"Ever since you stopped in front of me on the plane, you're the only thing on my mind. When I first saw you, my heart started pounding in my chest and my mouth became so dry I could barely talk. My body reacted so fiercely to yours that I was embarrassed, afraid you would notice my body's reaction when you took the baby from me. When you left to return to your seat, I felt as if part of me had been torn away."

"Me too," she confessed. "I'm afraid," she told him.

He pulled her gently into his arms. "What about?"

"This is all happening too fast." Her eyes looked deeply into his, her fear covering her face for him to see.

He stroked his hand along her face. "We'll take our time."

"What will your family think about our relationship?" she asked hesitantly, unsure what his answer would be.

"I guess they would be happy for us," he said, smiling at what his brothers would say about this relationship.

"Wouldn't they be a bit surprised we were planning to get married after knowing each other for only one day?" she inquired, her eyebrow raised in worry.

"Probably. Lindsay, I don't see how that would be a problem." He was confused, wondering if she was saying she didn't want to marry him.

She pulled away to look at him. "Let me ask you a question. Would you consider yourself a rich man?"

Casey's eyes darkened as he studied her. Where was she going with this question? "You know that I'm part owner of a company and you've seen the size of my house. You know I have money. So why do you ask?" Did she want to marry him just for his money? She didn't look the type of woman who would marry a man for that reason, but then what did women look like who would marry a man just for his money.

"If we were to get married, your family and friends would assume I was marrying you for your money."

"I could tell them I was marrying you for your money," he teased lightheartedly, wiggling his eyebrows at her at his joke.

"Are you?" she asked, closely watching him.

Her words angered him. "You think I am?" he shouted his question at her.

"How do I know! I barely know you," she shouted back.

He thought for a second, trying to comprehend what she was implying. "So, you're saying you have money?"

"You really don't know who I am, do you?" She wasn't surprised, thinking most men weren't familiar with writers of romance novels.

"You told me you were Lindsay Haggard. Was that a lie?" His thoughts were bouncing wildly in his head.

She didn't know how to explain that she was a famous author. "Let me try to explain. You mentioned that you saw some of my books at your sister's home."

"That's right. So?" He wasn't sure where she was going with this.

"How many do you think you saw?"

"I didn't count them," he replied frigidly, "I was trying to take care of burying my sister and her husband.

What does the number of books have to do with anything?" he asked roughly.

His tone hurt her feelings, but she understood his frustration. "I'm sorry about your family. What I should have said is that I have approximately seventy published books. All of them have been on the best seller list for at least for a week, but most of them have been on it longer," she explained.

His eyebrows lifted in surprise as he stared at her. "You're saying you're a famous writer?" he asked in awe.

"Yes. I've made a lot of money over the last five years. Right now, I have over one million dollars in the bank."

"Then I can quit my job and live off your income," he teased with a wicked smirk.

She laughed at his joking. "I guess."

"I'll tell you what we'll do. I'll have a lawyer draw up a prenuptial agreement and . . ." he began.

She put her hand on his arm. "Casey, you don't have to do that. I really don't think you're after my money."

"I know, but this is what needs to be done, this way we're both protected no matter what happens. What do you think?" He held his breath as he waited for her reply.

"I think it sounds like a good plan." She wasn't worried about him trying to get her money, but this way, it was protected just in case.

"Now all we have to do is to decide when we want to have the wedding."

She couldn't believe she was actually going to marry this man, but then she frowned. What if she what she felt was just lust for him and not love? She jumped when Casey seized her hand and pulled her into his arms.

Casey had seen her frowned and was concerned to what had caused it. He wanted to comfort her, as his need to touch her was so great that he reached out and pulled her into a tight hug. "Are you getting cold feet? You want to cancel the wedding?"

Lindsay felt tears forming in her eyes and tried to prevent them from falling. "I don't know. What if this isn't love that I feel for you? What if I'm just lusting after you?"

Casey chuckled. "Honey, if you are lusting after me, then I hope you never quit."

She hit his arm. "I'm serious. I don't want a loveless marriage."

"I'm sorry. I shouldn't tease you about your feelings." He wiped her tears away with his thumbs. "I don't think you're just lusting after me, but just in case you are, we'll set a date for the wedding for some time in June. That will give us two and a half months to become better acquainted, if during that time you change your mind about marrying me, we'll cancel the wedding. Does that make you feel better?"

"Yes, it does." She leaned over and gave him a quick kiss. "Casey, when are we going to tell your family about us?" she asked, as she was engulfed into Casey's arms.

"We'll have them all over for dinner and tell them. Now, let's get started working on your novel."

"What about that experiment we were going to do?" Her eyes twinkled at him as she thought about making love to him again.

"Maybe we should go to my bedroom before we start," he said, pulling her into his arms.

She laughed. "So, you think I won't be able to resist your charms?"

"No, I won't be able to resist yours." His mouth latched onto hers and his lips began making love to hers. His body wanted hers so badly he was in physical pain, he quickly dragged his lips from hers, clutched her hand, and pulled her after him.

As soon as they entered the bedroom, Casey began undressing her. "No, let me," she said, pushing his hands away. "You work on your clothes," she groaned breathlessly.

Casey laughed at her impatience. "Honey, I'm not going anywhere."

The only place he did go was to take her to heaven and back. After they made love again, they dressed, and went downstairs to start working on Lindsay's novel.

Casey was toiling on the research Lindsay wanted, but stopped as he watched in awe as her fingers flew across the keys on her computer. "I thought you were having writer's block?"

She stopped and looked up at him. "I was, but it seems to have left me."

"That's apparent as you've worked nonstop for the last twenty minutes."

"Well, sometimes I can't stop the flow once it has started. I want to get as much down as I can before Austin wakes up."

The couple spent the rest of the day working in the office, stopping only to eat and take care of the baby. By bedtime, Lindsay was exhausted, but satisfied with all the work they had accomplished. At this rate, her book would be finished in no time at all. After feeding the baby at nine, she started into her bedroom, but Casey stopped her by putting his hand on her arm.

"What's the matter?" She was confused to why he had stopped her.

"I think you should sleep with me," he said, and then his lips descended to hers.

His words warmed her heart, but his kisses heated her the most. Before she knew it, they were in his bed making love again. It felt right, as if she was meant to be with this man, to be his wife and to take care of Austin, but she was worried how she was going to tell her in-laws that she was marrying a man she barely knew.

"Lindsey, quit your worrying. It will all work out for us."

She turned to him in the darkness of the room. "How do you know I'm worrying?"

"You keep sighing, and by the sound of it, I figured you were worrying. What is it? What has upset you?"

"I was thinking about my in-laws. How can I tell them that I'm not grieving for their son any longer?" her anguished could be heard in her voice.

"Don't say that to them, instead tell them something less hurtful. Tell them that you've found someone to fill the emptiness caused by their son's death. You don't have to tell them all the dirty details." He found her face with his hand and stroked it. "I'm sure they'll understand, maybe not right away, but eventually. You're a young woman, I'm sure they don't expect you to never remarry."

"I guess you're right."

"Go to sleep. We'll talk more in the morning."

Lindsay let her mind go blank and was soon sound asleep, that is until Austin woke for his next feeding.

CHAPTER FIVE

Mariah and Evan were quiet on the drive home, both thinking that once they got home, she would stop taking her birth control pills and they would start working on creating their own baby. She wouldn't get pregnant tonight, but hopefully soon.

Mariah saw Evan's forlorn expression. "Evan is something wrong?" she asked as they walked into the house.

"My sister is dead and all I can think about is making love to you." He looked at her with tears in his eyes. "Does that make me a bad person?"

"Of course not. Alexandra and Clayton wouldn't expect us to quit living."

"I know, but still, I think I should be thinking more about them and less about myself. We need to make arrangements for them."

Mariah took his hand and squeezed it. "I'm sure Casey will see to it."

"I'm the oldest. I feel I should be doing it." He had always been the one in charge that is until Casey started his own company, then asked his family to work for him.

"Call him first if it will make you feel better."

Evan reached over and pulled her to him. "Thanks," he whispered, then brought her lips to his.

They entered the living room and Mariah went directly to their answering machine. There was a message from Casey, which said the funeral would be Monday at one.

"I'm not sure what I should do about work. Alexandra had a lot of friends at Clemmens' Manufacturing before she married Clayton," he said, walking towards their bedroom. His sister had been Chandler's assistant before she met her husband and moved away.

"Why don't you close down the office Monday at noon? That way anyone who wants to go to the funeral will be able to, and those who don't want to, don't have to go."

"That's a good suggestion," he said as he put his suitcase on the bed and opened it. "I think I'll call Morgan."

Sex wasn't mentioned again, so Mariah left the bedroom and went into the living room so Evan wouldn't see her disappointment.

He sat down on the bed and dialed his brother's number, and the phone was picked up on the second ring.

"Hello?"

"Morgan, it's Evan. Have you heard from Casey?"

"I wasn't home when he called, but I do know about the funeral for Alexandra and Clayton."

"I hope that won't cause a problem for you," he asked, thinking about their father.

"Evan, Alexandra was our sister. If Casey wants to have her buried next to Mom and his father, then that's fine with me."

"You don't think Dad will want to be buried next to Mom?" Evan asked nervously.

"If he did, then he shouldn't have divorced her and left us to run off with that younger woman," Morgan replied angrily.

He understood Morgan's anger. "Have you talked to Dad?"

"No, and I don't plan to. Have you kept in touch with him?"

"No, it's been several years since I've heard from him. Do you know if Chandler has heard from him?"

"I don't think so, if he has, he hasn't mentioned it to me."

"Have you talked to Chandler since Casey called?"

"Yes. He's fine with them being buried next to Mom. Evan, I really must go. I have a business meeting in St. Louis. Hailey is going with me and I still have to get her things packed. I'll see you Monday at the funeral."

"Have a safe trip. Bye, Morgan." Evan hung up the phone and went to search for Mariah. When he found her, he told her about Morgan's trip.

"Did you tell him about us finding Lindsay?" she asked excitedly.

"I didn't even think about it. We can tell him when he gets back to town. Now, where were we?" he asked, pulling her into his arms.

* * *

Lesley Arrington was in Columbia, Missouri for a three-day writer's convention. She had written a book and was trying to get it published, and this program promised to help writers achieve this goal. The meeting was over for the day, but there were still two more days before she could return to St. Louis.

It always made her nervous to speak in front of a group of people. She hadn't slept well last night for worrying about today, as she had been on the agenda today to speak about her novel. She was glad she didn't have to drive home today because a fierce late March snowstorm was hitting the city and several people in the meeting mentioned that I-70, the highway she would have used to go home, had been closed.

She went through the lobby as she returned to her hotel room, and as she passed the check-in desk, her stomach growled loudly. She immediately looked around to make sure no one had heard it, then stopped when she saw a little girl, who was maybe four or five looking at her.

Lesley could tell the child had been crying, but now she had a smile on her face as she looked at Lesley. Her eyes followed up the little girl's arm to the hand she was holding, then swiftly looked up the other arm, to the most gorgeous man she's ever seen. She blushed when she saw that he had a wide grin on his face as he stared at her.

"Excuse me. I didn't eat much lunch today," she said to the pair.

"Then you better go have some dinner before you pass out." Morgan forced the coherent words out of his mouth as he stared at the beautiful woman in front of him. He was so distracted by her beauty that he hadn't noticed her resemblance to his sister-in-law, so it never occurred to him that she could be one of Mariah's sisters, especially since he wasn't aware Mariah had any sisters or that she was searching for them.

"I will." Lesley waved to the little girl and strolled away. She went into her room and quickly removed her suit and put on a pair of slacks and a cream-colored sweater. When she walked back through the lobby, the same man and child were still there, but this time she could tell something was wrong as the man held the sobbing child. "Excuse me. Is the child sick?" Lesley was a nurse and wanted to help if she could.

"No, the highway has been closed. We came here to rent a room for the night, but there aren't any available. We'll have to sleep in the lobby and Hailey is upset about it."

"I'm sorry." Lesley put her hand out to him. "I'm Lesley Arrington. I have an extra bed in my room that I'd be willing to share."

Her offer shocked him. People didn't do this sort of thing anymore because there were too many criminals were out there looking to hurt someone as beautiful as this woman was. "I'm Morgan Clemmens and this is my daughter, Hailey." He took hold of Lesley's hand, and gave it a tight squeeze. "Weren't you taught not to let strangers in your hotel room?"

"My mother might have mentioned it to me a time or two," she teased as she smiled at him. In reality, her mother really didn't give a damn what she did. "If you give the hotel clerk all your personal information, just in case you go postal, I'm sure I'll be safe."

He couldn't believe this stranger had offered them a bed in her room. "I don't know how to thank you," he told her sincerely, setting Hailey on the ground.

"Don't worry about it."

Hailey ran up to Lesley. "Can I sleep with you in your bed?" she inquired excitedly.

Lesley knelt beside her. "If your father says yes, you're more than welcomed to share my bed."

Hailey threw her arms around Lesley's neck. "If he says yes, can you be my mommy too?" she innocently asked, her eyes bright with left over tears.

Hailey's movement threw Lesley off balance, but Morgan was close and quickly grabbed her back to prevent her from falling. He took hold of her hand to help her up, completely unprepared for the electrical tremor that had shot through him at their contact.

When the man took hold of her hand to help her up, she felt a sharp, electrical current shoot through her. She tried to remove her hand from his, but he just tightened his grip, so she gave up trying. "Thank you," she said the man, then turned and smiled at the child. "Thank you for the offer, but I don't think I can."

"Why not?" the child asked, her naive eyes staring at Lesley.

Lesley turned back to the man. "You want to help me here?"

He shook his head at her. "No, I would like to know why not too," he teased, smiling a sexual-filled grin at her.

"Gee thanks," she replied sarcastically, then looked back at his young child. "I'm sorry, but in order to be your mother, your father and I would have to be married," she said, thinking that would be the end of that.

"I like weddings," Hailey replied excitedly. "Can I be the flower girl?" she inquired sweetly.

Lesley didn't know what to say next to the little girl. "I'm sorry, but I can't be your mother." She pulled her hand free of his. "I'm going to dinner now. Do you two want to join me?"

"Yes," Hailey said, jumping up and down in front of her. "I want a hot dog."

"Let dinner be my treat," Morgan told her. When she nodded in acknowledgment to his offer, he bent down to retrieve their two pieces of luggage.

"Do you want to put your suitcases in my room now or later?"

"Be better to do it now. Otherwise we would have to take it to the dining room with us."

The three of them turned and went in the direction Lesley had just come. When she reached her room, she opened the door, and Morgan sat the luggage inside the room.

"I need to call my family in Kansas City to let them know Hailey and I are safe. Is it all right if I use your room phone before we go to dinner?" he asked.

"You can, but why don't you use my cell phone instead. I have free long distance, that way you won't have to pay an expensive phone charge."

"Thank you." He took the phone she handed him. "It will just take a few minutes."

"Hailey and I will use the rest room while you make your call." Lesley took hold of the child's hand and they went into the bathroom. She closed the door, but she could still hear Morgan talking, curious to whom he was talking.

"It's Morgan, Hailey and I are in Columbia. I-70 has been closed and we're staying at a hotel until they reopen it."

The room was quiet for a few seconds, then Lesley heard Morgan say he would call before they started for home. She opened the door and stepped into the room just as he disconnected the phone.

"Thank you. I'm sure my brothers wouldn't have worry about us, but my sister-in-law would have."

"How many brothers do you have?"

"I have three."

"No sisters?"

"We did, but she and her husband were killed recently."

"I'm so sorry. Did they have any children?"

"They had a baby boy."

"How sad." Lesley noticed tears in his eyes and decided not to ask any more questions about his sister, as she knew just how he felt about losing a sister. "I'm ready for dinner."

"Me too," Hailey told her.

"Let's go then."

She closed the door and they went to the dining room. They had a nice meal and while they ate, they became better acquainted. Lesley learned he was an electrician, lived in Kansas City, and his wife had been dead for two years. She told him she was a nurse by day and an unpublished writer by night. Her mother had once been a writer, but hadn't written anything lately because now, all she did was drink. She lived in St. Louis and had a boyfriend named Conrad. She was surprised that even after mentioning her boyfriend, Morgan didn't appear to lose interest in her.

When Hailey began rubbing her eyes, they decided to return to Lesley's room. Morgan carried his daughter to the room, and she was asleep by the time they reached it. When they entered the room, Lesley hurried to the closest bed to pull down the bedspread, then Morgan laid the sleeping child down on the bed.

"I'll get her nightgown," Morgan whispered, stepping away from Lesley.

Lesley went to the child and began undressing her, pretending this was her little girl. When Morgan handed her the gown, she put it on the child, then covered her with the blankets.

"I really do thank you for sharing your room," he said, looking down at his sleeping daughter.

"I'm glad I could help. If you don't mind, I'll use the bathroom to change into my nightgown, then I'm going to bed." She jumped when Morgan reached out and gripped her arm. "What?" Her first thought was he was going to attack her, and it was then that she realized that he hadn't given the hotel clerk his information.

"I'm sorry," he said, quickly letting go of her arm. "Do you have to go to bed so soon? It isn't even nine yet."

"I didn't get much sleep last night and I have a big day tomorrow," she said, stepping away from him.

He quickly reached for her and pulled her to him. As he brought her body against him, she put her hand on his chest to stop him. When she looked into his eyes and saw his desire, she began to panic. "I don't know what you're thinking you're doing, but I believe it would be best if you let go of me."

"I will, but first I'm going to kiss you."

Before Lesley could do anything to stop him, he pulled her tightly against his chest, pinning her arms between his. Her stomach tightened in terror, then jumped when his lips slowly touched hers.

She was expecting just a short kiss, but once his lips touched hers, she relaxed, and the kiss deepened as his tongue began making love to hers. She hadn't ever had a kiss affect her quite like this one had. When she felt his hand transfer from her waist to her breast, she jerked back, but he didn't release her. Her whole body was tingling with sexual fire and it scared her, but she knew if he wanted to make love to her, she would let him.

According to her high school sex education class, it was her safe time and she couldn't get pregnant.

"I don't care you have a boyfriend. I want you," he whispered into her ear.

Lesley couldn't find the words to tell him she wanted him too. Instead, she returned her lips to his, moving her arms around his waist. One minute they were dressed beside the bed, and the next minute, they were on it together naked.

Not once did the thought of Conrad enter Lesley's mind. He was a nice man, but his kisses hadn't ever made her feel this alive. As Morgan continued to make love to her, the fire in her persisted, and she welcomed it.

Afterward they made love, Morgan pulled her against him and kissed her. "That was wonderful. I was afraid I might be a bit rusty in the love making department, but by your vocal response, I guessed I remembered enough to satisfy you."

She blushed at his comment. She knew she should feel guilty for what had just happened, but she didn't. In fact, she was thinking she would like a repeat performance. "You did all right, I guess," she teased, hoping he would make love to her again.

"What? What is that supposed to mean?" He had a hurt expression on his face, not realizing she was teasing him.

"I believe you could use some more practice," she cooed into his ear. When he shifted on top of her abruptly, she let out a soft squeal, then his lips found hers and the loving began once again. She felt as if she was in heaven as he made love to her a second time.

The next morning, Lesley woke up before the alarm went off. She grabbed her clothes and went into the bathroom to get ready for her day. Even if they wanted to have a romantic relationship, they lived on either side of Missouri, which was at least a four hours trip between the two cities, and that was on a good day.

Lesley was mad at herself for even thinking he would want to see her again. Just because they had sex, it didn't mean he would want to have a relationship with her. She stepped out of the bathroom, closing the door behind her.

Lesley looked over at the bed and saw both of her guests were still sleeping. She wanted to leave him a note, so she searched her purse for a something to write on. When she didn't find anything, she snatched a deposit slip from her checkbook and grabbed a pen from the small table in her room. She wrote that she would be back around five, then left it on the table near the door. She stopped at the bed, leaned down, and kissed Hailey on her cheek. "Bye sweet Hailey. I'll see you later." She opened the door and hurried out. Just then, the heater kicked on and as she closed the door; her note flew under the bed.

CHAPTER SIX

Morgan woke when he heard the door closed and quickly looked around the room to see what had woken him. For a split second, he didn't know where he was, but once he realized he was in Lesley's hotel room, a wide grin covered his face as he remembered their lovemaking. Seeing the bathroom door closed, he figured Lesley was in there getting ready for the day.

He got out of bed and started the coffee pot that was on the counter next to the sink. He dressed, then poured himself a cup, then sat down at the table to drink it while he waited for Lesley to come out of the bathroom. He was still sitting at the table when Hailey woke up.

"Hi Daddy."

"Good morning, sweetheart." He stood, went to his daughter, and picked her up. "Did you sleep well last night?"

"Yes, but I need to go potty."

"You'll have to wait; Lindsay is in there."

"No, she isn't."

Morgan frowned at her. "What are you talking about?"

"She kissed me, said she would see me later, and then left."

Morgan threw open the bathroom door expecting to see Lesley, but instead, he found it empty. He felt hurt that she hadn't woken him before she'd left. Maybe last night hadn't meant as much to her as it had him. While Morgan helped his daughter get dress, he listened to the morning news. The newscaster said that I-70 had been reopened all the way to Kansas City, but another storm was anticipated to hit the area later in the day.

Morgan was torn to what to do. Part of him wanted to wait for Lesley to return, but the other part knew he had to leave for home as soon as possible, as his brothers would never forgive him if he missed their sister's funeral.

He wrote Lesley a quick note on an old receipt he had in his pocket, leaving her his phone number and a short message as to why they had left before she returned. He laid the note on the same bedside table that Lesley had, and when they opened the door to leave for home, it too flew under the bed.

When Morgan returned home, he called Casey to let him know he was home and would at the funeral on Monday.

* * *

What a day! Lesley didn't think today's meeting would ever end. She returned to her room, quickly unlocking it, and stepping inside. The smile on her face promptly disappeared when she saw the room was empty. Her eyes rapidly searched the room for some sign of her guests from last night, but she didn't see one thing that had belong to the Clemmens.

She shut the door and sat down on the first bed. Tears formed as she realized they had left without even saying goodbye. Her heart broke as she thought about what had happened between them last night. Hadn't it meant anything to him at all? "Fine," she said to the empty room, then she angrily wiped her tears away, but they continued to fall as she flopped backwards onto the bed.

The phone rang and she quickly grabbed it, thinking it would be Morgan, but it was the coordinator of convention calling to say tomorrow's program had been cancelled due to the weather. Lesley packed her bags and hurried out of the room for home.

When she returned to St. Louis, she called Conrad and told him that she needed to see him, as she couldn't continue to see him now, she'd been involved with another man. When he arrived at her door, she let him in but didn't let him kiss her.

Conrad gave her a puzzled good. "Is something wrong?" Did she know that he'd been seeing another woman and was planning on breaking up with her?

"I'm sorry Conrad, but I don't want to see you anymore," she said softly.

Conrad nodded. "We're just not right for each other, are we?" he asked, sadly looking at her.

"No, we aren't. I'm sorry."

He gave her a weak smile. "No need to be. Neither one of us has that special feeling for the other to make this relationship work."

"You've felt it too?" She was relieved, as she hadn't wanted to hurt him.

"Yes. I was coming over here to tell you it was over because I've met someone else, but you beat me to it."

Lesley leaned over and kissed his cheek. "You've been a good friend and I wish you luck with your new friend."

"Thanks."

Conrad left and she slowly closed the door. She was depressed breaking up with a man she'd been dating for several months but knew she had done the right thing. After meeting Morgan, she realized she couldn't ever be happy with Conrad.

* * *

Lindsay decided it would be better if she didn't go to the funeral, so she'd stayed at the house with Austin.

The funeral was a sad and solemn occasion as the four brothers said good-bye to their sister. After the service, the family visited together a few moments talking about their sister and her husband.

It wasn't until after Morgan left with Hailey that the conversation turned to the subject of Mariah's sisters. It was then Mariah told the remaining three brothers' stories about Lindsay and their other two sisters being separated during their childhood.

Casey didn't mention anything to Mariah about his new relationship with Lindsay, wanting to wait until Lindsay was with him before he did. Instead, he told the family about Lindsay being a well-known published writer and that he was helping her with her research. "Mariah, can you and Evan come to dinner tonight?"

"Of course."

"We need to talk to you both," he replied, but not mentioning that Lindsay didn't know anything about him inviting them for dinner.

"What time do you want us?"

Casey quickly thought how much time Lindsay would need to prepare a dinner party she didn't know anything about. "How does six o'clock sound?" he asked nervously.

Mariah sense something wasn't right here and gave at her brother-in-law a questioning look, but he looked away, then she turned towards her husband. "Evan, does that sound good to you?"

"It depends on what she's fixing. If it's something I love, I'm ready to go now," Evan said jokingly.

Casey laughed a forced chuckle. "I don't think she's quite ready for you to show up this soon."

Mariah studied Casey for a moment, suddenly realizing what wasn't right with this situation. "Casey Pennay, don't tell me Lindsay doesn't know anything about your invitation."

"Well," he hedged, refusing to look at Mariah.

"Come on, tell me the truth," she demanded.

"The truth is that she said she wanted you to come over one night for dinner, but not which night."

"We can make it some other time."

"No, I want it to be tonight." He was anxious to tell Mariah about his relationship with her sister, as until he did, he would feel like a teenager sneaking behind his parents' back.

"Won't she be worn out taking care of Austin all day?"

"I'll go home and make her take a nap and I'll help her with dinner."

Evan grabbed hold of his wife's waist. "We'll be there at six. Come on woman, let's you and I go home so we can work on our little project."

Casey started to ask what project he was referring to, but when he saw Mariah blush, he realized what his brother meant. He hurried home so he could tell Lindsay about their dinner company. When he entered the house, he heard Austin crying and followed the sound. When he reached the top of the stairs, he heard Lindsay talking to the baby.

"Little man just let me finish putting on this clean diaper, then you'll get your afternoon snack," Lindsay told the crying child. He felt a bit warm to her but thought it must have been because of the heavy of blanket she had on him.

The crying quit, so Casey figured that Austin was nursing. He stepped into the room and watched as Lindsay nursed the baby. "Someday you'll be nursing our child at your breast."

Lindsay jumped at the sound of his voice. "Casey, you startled me," she said, her hand resting on her chest. "I didn't hear you come in."

"I'm sorry," he replied slowly, trying to decide how to tell her about his dinner invitation to Mariah and Evan. He felt guilty now for inviting them for dinner without talking to her first, as just looking at her, he could tell she was exhausted.

"Casey, is something wrong?" She didn't know him well, but something told her he wanted to tell her something.

"I invited Evan and Mariah over for dinner," he said, then just stared at her.

"Tonight?" Her eyes filled with panic.

"Yes, but just looking at you, I can tell you're too tired to be fixing a big dinner for guests."

"Maybe if I took a nap while this young man slept, then we could fix dinner together."

"You're not angry that I invited them without asking you first?" He was surprised, thinking she would be, since most women he knew would be.

She smiled at him. "No, we need to talk to them about us and the sooner, the better."

"Can I take a nap with you?" he asked, then gave her an ornery wink.

"Only if you promise you'll behave yourself."

"You're so heartless."

"I'll make it up to you later tonight when we go to bed."

"It's a deal."

After a good nap, Lindsay felt rested, and was ready to start on dinner. With Casey's help, they fixed lasagna, a salad, and garlic toast. When the doorbell rang, the timer showed they had five minutes before dinner was ready. Casey went to let them in, while Lindsay filled the glasses with ice and water. Mariah came into the kitchen just as the timer went off.

"You have great timing," Lindsay teased her sister.

"Is there anything I can do to help?"

"Round up the guys and we'll be ready."

"What about Austin?"

"He's still sleeping."

"Has he been sleeping long?"

Lindsay looked at the clock on the wall. "He should be waking up any time now, but hopefully, we'll be done with dinner by the time he wakes."

Soon the four of them were busy filling their plates, Casey said grace, and then they started eating. Mariah kept looking between her sister and Casey, waiting for one of them to say why she and Evan were here tonight, but neither one of them said anything. By the time they were finishing their meal, Mariah was so frustrated she kicked Evan under the table and gave him a look to say she wanted him to ask why they were there.

"Casey was there some reason you wanted us here tonight?" he asked, seeing Mariah grinning at him out of the corner of his eye.

Casey looked at Lindsay, then back at his brother. "Yes, there is."

Before he could say another word, a baby's cry was heard from the monitor.

"I'll go tend to him and be right back," Lindsay said, noticing Mariah's disappointed look by the interruption.

"We'll wait for you."

The three of them started talked about Austin when Lindsay was out of the room. A few seconds later, Lindsay's scream was heard over the monitor and Casey, Evan, and Mariah jumped up from the table and ran from the room. When they arrived, Lindsay was holding a convulsing baby in her arms.

Lindsay's tear-filled eyes looked at them. "Help me. I don't know what to do," she sobbed.

Casey's cell phone rang just as he was about to take the baby from her. He wasn't going to answer it, but when he looked at the caller ID, he saw that it was Morgan. If anyone knew about babies and fevers, it was Morgan, as Hailey had been sick frequently when she was a baby.

"Morgan, Austin is having a convulsion. What should we do?"

"Is he hot to the touch?"

Casey touched the child. "Yes, he's burning up."

"Get a washcloth wet with cool water; apply it to his forehead and neck and put lukewarm water on the rest of his body. Whatever you do, don't use cold water or rubbing alcohol because it may make it worse. After the seizure quits, give him some baby acetaminophen and get him to the hospital as quick as you can."

"Thanks, we'll keep in touch."

While Lindsay held the infant, the rest of the family did as Morgan said. When the seizure was over, they headed for Casey's car because of the baby's car seat. Since Casey was too upset to drive, Evan drove them to the hospital. Mariah sat up front with her husband, while Casey and Lindsay got into the back seat with the baby.

Lindsay cried on the way to the hospital, telling the family that he had felt warm when she had laid him down after his last feeding and felt guilty for not giving him something then to reduce the fever.

The nurses in the emergency room took the baby right in and started immediate treatment on him. Everyone was relieved to found out the high fever had been caused by an ear infection. The doctor reassured Lindsay that she hadn't done anything wrong and that Austin wouldn't have any lasting complications due to the convulsion.

Once they were back at the house, Casey wanted her to put Austin back in his crib, but she refused to let him out of her sight. They all went into the living room and sat down with Austin in Lindsay's arms.

"I know this has been a full evening, but I want you both to know that Lindsay and I are going to get married," Casey told their guests.

Mariah looked over at her sister, then looked back at Casey. "Why?" she asked him.

"What do you mean, why? Why does any couple get married?" he asked her hatefully.

"You're telling me that you and Lindsay are in love?" Mariah was shocked by his statement.

"Why do you find that so hard to believe?" he screamed, angry at Mariah thoughtless question.

"You've just met. Besides, you should only get married for the right reason."

"What would be a wrong reason?" he inquired, outraged with his sister-in-law for the third degree they were getting from her.

"Casey, Mariah doesn't want you two to be getting married just because of Austin," Evan inserted into the conversation. "You should love each other."

Lindsay smiled over at her sister. "Mariah, I know it's a shock for you, but we have fallen in love."

Mariah didn't want to ask her sister, but she didn't have any choice, she had to say what was on hers and Evan's mind. "So, you're saying you aren't marrying Casey for his money."

Lindsay was hurt by her sister's comment, but part of her realized she was trying to protect Casey. "Mariah, I plenty of my own money I don't need any of Casey's money."

"Really? Do you have as much as he has?"

She turned to look at Casey before responding. "I don't know how much he has in the bank, but I have one million dollars in my account."

Mariah was floored by Lindsay's statement. "What? How can you have that much money?"

"Mariah, let it drop. It really isn't any of our business why they want to get married," Evan said, touching her hand.

Lindsay turned to look at Evan. "Evan, it's all right." Then she looked back to her sister. "You know that I'm a published author, what you may not know is that I've sold a lot of books."

"I apologize for my comment. It's just that Casey has been my family for five years, and I haven't seen you for over twenty years. I don't know you anymore," she said, hoping her sister understood what she meant.

"Mariah, I understand your concern. For your information, Casey and I've talked about our money. We're going to protect both of our interest by having a prenuptial agreement, just in case the marriage doesn't last."

Evan stood. "Come on Mariah, I think it's time for us to go home."

"Thank you for dinner, I'm sorry for my rude comment."

Lindsay reached over, took hold of her sister's hand, and squeezed it. "Don't worry about it. I'm glad that you care enough for Casey to watch over him."

Casey and Lindsay walked their guests to the front door and waved good-bye to them as they drove away.

"That went well," Casey said, trying to keep a straight face.

"You think so?" She turned to look at him, not sure, if he meant what he'd said.

"At least Mariah didn't accuse me of marrying you for your money," he teased, his eyes twinkling.

Lindsay frowned at him. "Is that a good sign? Or does Mariah just trust you more than she does me?" she asked, with a touch of hurt in her voice.

He turned to her and pulled her into his arms. "Lindsay don't take it to heart. You and your sister are strangers."

"Her comment still hurt," she replied sadly.

"Let's go to bed and I'll try to think of a way to make it up to you."

"You're just trying to get me into trouble," she snickered.

He laughed loudly. "You sure do have my number. Next time I'll have to be more inventive."

She giggled. "I'll just have to keep on my toes when I'm around you."

"Sounds interesting. I've never tried *it* that way."

Lindsay lightly hit his arm. "The way you're going, you may never get *it* ever again."

"So, you think you can resist my charms," he teased.

She leaned against him, brought her lips to his, and kissed him. "Never."

CHAPTER SEVEN

May

"You two are so lucky to have found each other," Chandler said longingly, watching Evan and Mariah holding hand and smiling at each other.

"Chandler, you'll find someone," Mariah told him. "You're a handsome man, you shouldn't have any trouble finding a woman to love."

Chandler looked over at his brother, but Evan didn't say a word, instead he just simply shook his head. Even though his brother hadn't said anything, he knew what he meant, he hadn't told his wife anything concerning Chandler's problem.

He went to Mariah and took hold of her hands. "Mariah, thank you for your kind words, but I have a slight problem that most women don't tend to overlook."

Assuming he meant he had a small penis, Mariah eyes traveled down to his crotch, then jerked back up to his face as a reddish glow covered her face. "I didn't know. I just assumed you would be the same size as your brother."

When Chandler saw her glance to his groin and then her blushing face, he laughed loudly, giving her hand a tight squeeze. "No, that isn't my problem," he said, thinking back to his teenage years and the many times he and his brothers had compared their sexual organs. Out of the four of them, he had always been the biggest. "Mariah, when I was fifteen, I had the mumps."

Mariah's hands flew to her mouth as tears quickly formed in her eyes, for she knew that when older boys had mumps, they could become sterile because of their high fevers. "Chandler," she started, but the words she wanted to say to him wouldn't come. "Weren't you vaccinated against it?" she asked softly.

"I was, but I still got it." He pulled her into his arms. "Don't feel sorry for me. I may be sterile, but I'm still a healthy man with a good sex drive." He laughed at her teasing groan. "I'll find the right woman someday." He let go of her and stepped back. "I could always find a woman who already has children."

She nodded. "I'm sure you'll find her."

"Or there's always adoption," he said, giving her hand another squeeze.

"Yes, you're right," she replied, thinking of Casey and his desire to adopt their nephew. "You'll make a great father."

* * *

Whitney stared at the pregnancy test in her hand and frowned, as now she knew for sure she and the man from the hotel, had had unprotected sex that night. She knew she couldn't keep the baby as she was barely keeping her head financially above water now. With a baby in her life, she would definitely sink to the bottom.

Thank God, she thought of getting the man's business card before leaving his room, as she needed to contact him to tell him about the baby. Maybe he would want the infant, then she shook her head, as he wouldn't want to raise a baby on his own since his wife was gone. She wasn't sure what she should do regarding the baby, but she knew he still had the right to know he was going to be a father.

She wanted to call him but figured this was something she had to do in person. She got the man's business card out of her jewelry box, sat down at her computer to look up how to get to his home in Independence on the Internet.

She typed in his address and found it wouldn't take her more than half an hour to get to his house from her apartment. She figured there wasn't any time like the present, so she grabbed her purse, pulled out her car keys, and started towards his home. When she arrived at his house, she knocked on the man's door, then forced herself to swallow as she nervously waited for him to answer it. Even though she could hear footsteps coming to the door, she still jumped when the door opened.

"Yes?" Evan asked when he opened the door. The sun was shining into his eyes, so he couldn't make out the woman's face, and so he didn't recognize her as the woman from the bar.

"Evan, it's me, Whitney O'Rourke." Whitney just stared at the man when he acted as if he'd never seen her before. Didn't he recognize her? Had he forgotten about their night together? Had he been too drunk that night to remember taking her to bed?

"Lady if you're selling something, I'm not interested," he said unfriendly. Chandler was over and the two of them were watching an exciting movie he'd rented. All he wanted to do was to shut the door and return to his chair to watch the movie.

"Mr. Clemmens, maybe you don't remember me, but we had met while you were in Tulsa two months ago. We had sex and I'm here to tell you I'm pregnant with your baby."

Anger filled Evan's face. "Look here. I don't know what you're trying to pull, but I've never seen you before, so you're definitely aren't getting any money out of me."

"Fine, don't believe me," she shouted at him. "It doesn't much matter to me what you believe, but when this baby is born, I'll be back to have your DNA checked and then I'll prove to you this child is yours."

"What's going on here?" Chandler asked, joining his brother at the front door when he heard their loud angry voices. When he looked outside, he was surprised to see a woman who reminded him of Mariah, only younger.

Whitney looked at the man who had joined them at the door, and by the looks of him, she figured he was probably Evan's younger brother. "A few months ago, Evan and I met at a bar in Tulsa. We had too much to drink and when I woke the next morning, we were in bed together. Now I'm expecting his baby."

"Chandler, she's lying. I never saw this woman before," Evan insisted, hoping his brother would believe him.

Chandler put out his hand. "I'm Chandler Clemmens, Evan's younger brother. Why don't you come into the house so we can talk about this?"

"She's knows I have money and is just here to blackmail me with her lies. I don't know why she's saying she is having my baby. I told you, I've never seen her before today," he shouted at his brother, praying that she was lying because otherwise that meant that he'd been unfaithful to Mariah.

"How do you explain how I got this?" Whitney pulled Evan's business card out of her purse and showed it to him.

Evan looked down at the card in her hand. Was it the card that had come up missing during his last business trip? He took it from her and turned it over. Sure enough, it was his missing card, but that didn't prove they had sex. She shifted, causing the sunlight to be blocked by her head and he got his first good look at her. He quickly realized that she did look familiar to him, then his mouth dropped open, as he was astonished of how much she looked like Mariah. He looked at his brother and then back to her. "I believe I remember you now, but I don't remember sleeping with you."

"Evan, why don't we go into the living room so that we can discuss this rationally. Your neighbors don't need to know all your dirty laundry."

Evan stepped back to let the woman enter the house and the three of them went to the living room. Evan sat down on loveseat, but Whitney stood there looking nervous at him.

"Please sit down," Chandler said to Whitney. He waited until she sat down on the couch, then he sat down next to Evan before he spoke. "Now start at the beginning."

While looking between Evan and Chandler, Whitney slowly explained everything she could remember from that night to the two men, and the longer she talked, the more she realized Evan really didn't remember their night together. She couldn't blame him since she didn't much of it either.

"I'm a married man. I love my wife, I wouldn't have had sex with you," he insistent franticly, tears threatening to fall.

"The way you talked about her that night, I got the impression that she was dead. You kept saying you'd lost her."

"We had a big fight, I thought our marriage was over, so I was drinking away my sorrows. Now my marriage really will be over when Mariah finds out I've been unfaithful. The worst part is I don't even remember going to bed with you," he moaned, putting his head into his hands.

Whitney could feel his pain. "I'm sorry. I don't want to hurt your marriage. I just wanted you to know I was expecting your baby."

"Are you positive it's mine?" he asked looking at her, hoping she would say she wasn't.

"Yes, I'm positive. I need to know whether you want to keep the baby or not. If you don't want it, I'm going to put the baby up for adoption after its born."

"No!" Evan yelled at her, jumping off the loveseat and walking to where she was sitting. "You will not put our baby up for adoption," he stated angrily. "Mariah and her sisters were separated from each other when she was a child and it about killed her. I won't do that to a child of mine." He studied her for a few seconds. "You look to be the motherly type, why don't you want the baby?"

"I didn't say I didn't want the child, but I'm barely making ends meet as it is. I can't afford to raise the baby on my own."

"We'll find a way to work through this," Evan told her as he said down next to her and clasped her hand in his. He had to find a way to solve this problem, but his troubled mind couldn't think of a single solution to this dilemma.

"Evan, we'll think of something." Chandler told his brother.

"There has to be something we can do," he muttered, even though he thought the situation was hopeless.

"If you could afford to pay child support, then maybe I could keep the baby. If you wanted to see the child, we could work out some sort of visiting arrangement."

Evan nodded. "Yes, that could work. We should obtain a lawyer and make everything legal."

Chandler moved over to the couch, sat down on the other side of Whitney, took hold of her hand, and smiled. "Or you could marry me," he quickly inserted into the conversation. When Whitney turned to stare at Evan's brother, he simply smiled at her.

"What?" She was shocked by his comment. "You can't be serious."

"Of course, I can. Will you marry me?" he asked, praying that she would say yes, then he would be a father to his brother's child.

The man did look sincere, but she couldn't understand why he'd asked her to marry him. "Why would you want to marry me? You don't even know me." She was puzzled to why this good-looking man would want to marry her especially knowing she was pregnant by his brother.

"I don't want my brother's child to be taken away from us. I would make your child my heir."

"Why would you want to do that?" Whitney couldn't believe this man, a stranger, would propose to her. As she sat there staring dumbfounded at the attractive man, she thought he was even better looking than his brother was. The thought of accepting his proposal caused her throat to tense up and she had forced herself to swallow.

Before Chandler could respond to her question, Evan spoke up. "Yes, that's would solve all our problems. If you married Chandler, we wouldn't have to say any to Mariah concerning any of this," Evan said excitedly.

Chandler quickly gave his brother a dirty look. "I can't believe you just said that. You want to lie to your wife? How do you think she would feel when she finds out that you've lied to her?"

"She doesn't ever have to find out," he said excitedly.

"I'm not going to lie to your wife," Whitney told Evan.

"Lie to me about what?" Mariah inquired, as she stepped into the room, surprising all three of them.

Three guilty looking people jumped out of their seats, turning to stare at her.

When Whitney looked at the woman who must be Evan's wife, she was astonished to see how much she was an older version of herself. No wonder Evan kept calling her by his wife's name.

When Mariah's eyes glimpse the young woman's face, she thought she'd seen a ghost. "Whitney is that you?" she asked, tears filling her eyes.

Whitney was shocked this stranger knew her name. "Yes?" she replied nervously. "How do you know my name? Do I know you?" This situation was getting worse by the minute, wondering if she was some distance relative of hers, as they looked enough alike that they could be sisters.

"I'm your sister, Mariah," she muttered tearfully as she rushed to her side, taking hold of her hand.

"What?" This couldn't be true; this woman couldn't be her sister. "You can't be my sister," she cried, a single tear dropped down her cheek. "All my sisters are dead. My adoptive mother told me so herself."

Mariah hurried to her, then wiped Whitney's tear away with her hand before pulling her into her arms, giving her a tight squeeze. "No, we aren't dead. Someone lied to you." She moved slightly away from Whitney and took hold of her hand. "Lindsay and I have just recently been reunited. Surprisingly, she has been living here in Kansas City."

"How wonderful! How does she look?" she asked, fighting to prevent herself from becoming hysterical at the realization that she was pregnant with her brother-in-law's baby. How much worst could this situation get?

"She looks great. Of course, she grown a bit since the last time I saw her."

Whitney forced a laugh at Mariah's joke. "What is she doing?"

"She's a published author and right now, she's helping Evan's brother Casey with their nephew who has lost both of his parents in March."

"How's sad. What about Lesley? Where is she?" she asked, clasping tightly to Mariah's hand. Being seven when she was taken from her sisters, she still remembered her childhood with her sisters.

"We don't know," she replied sadly. "We haven't been able to find her. Evan and Casey met Lindsay by accident on an airplane two months ago."

"Now all we need to do is to find Lesley, then we can be a family again. I still can't believe we've finally found each other."

"Me too. Now tell me, how come you're here if you didn't know about me?" Mariah asked, bringing the conversation back to why Whitney was here in the first place.

Whitney looked at the two men and then back at her sister. She was in trouble, deep trouble. Not only had she slept with and gotten pregnant by a married man, but that man was married to her sister. She looked back at Chandler, hoping that he would help her.

Chandler saw the panic in the young woman's eyes as she glanced at him a second time. He knew the situation just took a step from being an awful dilemma to a disaster. Chandler moved to Mariah and took hold of her hand. "Mariah, Whitney is here because . . ." he started.

Evan took hold of his brother's arm and pulled him away. "Let me. It's my responsibility to tell her."

"What is? What is going on here?" she yelled at them. "Will someone please tell me what is going on here?" She looked at Evan, then Chandler, then back to her husband.

"Mariah, I don't know how to tell you this, but . . ." his voice cracked. "First, let me say that I love you very much and I wouldn't ever purposely do anything to hurt you."

"I know that," she replied slowly, her eyes watching him closely.

"Please let me finish before you say anything. When we had that big fight a couple of months ago, I thought our marriage was over."

"Quit stalling and just tell me," she screamed at him.

"I'm trying to find the right words to explain what I've done," he choked out, as tears were causing his voice to quiver. Mariah looked petrified as she stared at him. "I was in the hotel bar the night before I was to come home, getting drunk, trying to forget you when Whitney joined me."

Whitney started crying as Evan started his confession, and Chandler pulled her into his arms trying to comfort her.

"At first, I thought Whitney was you. I don't remember anything about it, but apparently we went to bed together." He looked down at the floor, then back up at her. "Whitney's pregnant with my child." He held his breath as he waited for her to cuss him out, to hit him, and kick him out of their home, and out of her life.

Mariah turned away from him to look at her long-lost sister. She could understand how Evan in his drunken state had gone to bed with her, but what was Whitney's excuse. "Why did you go to bed with my husband?" she asked her sister, a hurt expression covered her face.

Whitney stared into Mariah's forlorn eyes. "I don't even remember going to his room. I don't have a good excuse for going to bed with him other than I thought he was a widower. He talked about how he'd lost you, I just assumed there had been death. One minute we were in the bar talking and the next minute I woke up in his bed." She couldn't stand to hurt her long-lost sister another second more.

"I'm so sorry. I just came to tell Evan about the baby and now that I have, I should be leaving." She moved out of Chandler's embrace, reached down to picked up her purse, then stood to leave the room, but Mariah stepped in front of her. "Please let me go. I think I've done enough damage here today."

"No. I lost you once, I'm not about to lose you again. I know how much our argument upset Evan. Add alcohol to the situation, it was bound to end bad. As much as we look alike, I can understand Evan going to bed with you. Evan is a handsome man, so I can identify with you having sex with him, especially if you thought he was unattached. We're all adults here; we'll find a way to work through all this. Does anyone have anything else to say regarding this matter?"

Chandler went to his sister-in-law and gave her a quick hug. "I have to say that I'm very proud of you for staying with your husband and forgiving your sister. I'm especially proud how well you're handling this tricky situation. I think you're a very smart and brave woman."

"I don't know about that since I feel I'm being selfish." The other three people in the room stared at her, confused by her words, but when no one said anything, she continued. "I don't want to lose my sister, who I haven't seen for twenty years, nor do I want to lose my husband who I love." Her eyes scanned the room, looking at Whitney, then Chandler, and lastly at her husband. "Particularly now that I've found out I'm pregnant."

"Hurrah," Evan hollered, seizing hold of his wife, giving her a tight hug, then he kissed her.

"I think it's time for me to leave. I'll give you my phone number and we can get together another time."

"Whitney, I wish you would stay. We have so much to talk about," Mariah said longingly.

"Yes, we do, but I think you and your husband need to talk alone first."

"She's right. I'll show her out and then I'll leave too," Chandler told them.

"Okay, but I don't want this to come between us," Mariah told her sister.

"If you can accept this situation, I guess I can too," she replied slowly.

"We'll find a solution to this problem that will satisfy us all."

"I hope so." Whitney looked sadly at her sister. "If you decide you don't ever want to see me again, I will understand."

Chandler looked over at Mariah and Evan. "You three need to discuss whether or not you want to tell the rest of the family about who's the father of Whitney's baby."

"I'll go along with whatever you two what to do," Whitney told them. "We could just keep it between the four of us or tell everyone. It doesn't matter to me."

"Let Mariah and me talk about this alone first. Then the four of us can sit down and make a rational decision," Evan told her.

Whitney simply nodded, then wrote down her phone number, and handed it Mariah. "Call me when you're ready to talk."

Mariah gave Whitney a quick hug. "I will."

Whitney left the room with Chandler, and when they reached the front door, she turned to him. "Thank you for you lovely marriage proposal. I can't accept it, but your kind offer did warm my heart."

"You're not getting off that easy. We're family now."

"That sounds nice," she said, smiling at him. "I've been alone too long."

"Tell me about your job."

"There isn't much to tell," she replied.

"What do you do at your job?" he asked, curious about this woman.

"I'm a data entry clerk," she said, but didn't elaborate on her position.

"Do you like it?" he asked, thinking that maybe they could hire her at Clemmens' Manufacturing, as it might help her financial structure.

"I guess it's all right. I like my co-workers, but I don't make much money. I had planned to go to college, but now I don't know what I'm going to do. What about you?"

"I work with my brothers at our family-owned manufacturing company."

"That sounds nice."

"It is, but my dream is to someday own some land and raise horses."

"Do you own a place now where you can raise them?"

"No, but maybe someday I will. Whitney, I know we just met each other, but I want you to know that I can't ever father a child."

"No," she cried, looking down at his crotch, then her eyes flew to his face as a blush covered her face.

Chandler forced to keep his grin from showing at her embarrassment. "It still works if that's what you were wondering," he teased, giving her a wink.

She shook her head. "That isn't any of my business," she muttered, horrified that he'd seen her looking at his manhood that lay behind the material of his pants.

"It would if we were to get married."

"Chandler, why do you want to marry me?" She still couldn't believe he'd proposed.

"Your baby will be half Clemmens. I want to be the child's father because this child is the closest possibility of me ever having a child of my own blood. Please, at least think about my proposal."

She gave him a reassuring smile. "We have over six months before the baby's born. Let's use that time getting to know one another to see if marriage is a possibility in our future."

Chandler seized her into a hug before she could turn away, and then quickly kissed her. If he hadn't been holding Whitney, the fireworks caused by his kiss would have caused her to collapse to the floor

When he finally did let go of her and stepped away, it took her several seconds before her muddled brain began working again. "That was nice," she said breathlessly.

"Thanks, I'm glad you enjoyed it," he replied with a childish grin, as he knew she felt the same elation as he had.

She shook her head as if the movement would clear her mind. "I need to be going."

"Can I have your phone number too?"

"Chandler, this is a serious matter. Evan and Mariah may choose not to have anything to do with me once they have a chance to talk."

"You don't know your sister like I do. She's not about to let you out of her life no matter what you've done with her husband," he said, without thinking of how his words would sound to her. He felt bad when she broke out in tears.

"Whitney, I'm so sorry. I didn't mean it to sound the way it did." He put his hand out and grabbed hold of hers, but Whitney pulled her hand away, sat down on the front porch, and started sobbing. "Is there a chance it be someone else's baby?" he asked as he sat down next to her, putting his arm around her shoulder.

She shook her head. "I woke up in his bed and he's the only man in my life for over a year. The worst part of it is that I don't have any memory of having sex with him."

"Maybe that's a good thing," he said softly, watching her expression at his statement.

"I don't see how," she cried, too embarrass to look at him.

"If neither of you remember being in bed together, then neither of you will have memories of that night to haunt you."

Whitney looked over at him as she thought about what he'd just said. "I guess you're right, but still I'm having my brother-in-law's baby. That sounds so horrible. How will I ever explain my child's conception to them?"

"As honest as possible, but I don't think you'll need to worry about that today, do you?"

She gave him a weak smile. "No, not today." She stood, and then looked down at him. "I need to be going."

"You will think over my proposal," he asked as he stood and moved next to her.

"Yes, I'll think about it," she told him, taking another step away.

Chandler grabbed hold of her hand before she could move away any farther. "I still need that phone number."

Whitney grabbed some paper out of her purse, wrote down her phone number, and handed it to him. "Bye, Chandler."

He wanted to offer her a job but was afraid she would interpret it wrong. Maybe once they got to know each other better, he could offer her a position with the company. Of course, if they got married, then she wouldn't have to work. "Bye, Whitney."

CHAPTER EIGHT

Evan pulled Mariah into his arms. "Mariah, how can you ever forgive what I've done?"

"Because I love you."

"But I had sex with another woman." His anguish filled his voice.

"I still forgive you," she said softly.

"To a woman who turns out to be your sister?"

"I guess I could have sex with one of your brothers," she teased, trying to ease some of the tension that was in the room.

"What?" he croaked, his face showing his disbelief at her comment.

Mariah quickly put her hand on his face. "Honey, I'm sorry. That was a bad joke. I forgive you because I'd rather have you in my life than live without you." She smiled at him. "Besides, we have a baby coming."

"I don't know if I'd be as understanding if our situations were reversed."

"Evan, I can understand how in your drunken and upset state you could have believed Whitney was me."

"But she wasn't you. I remember that she told me she wasn't. Even though I don't remember taking her back to my room, I still slept with her."

"Evan, you have to let this go. If you don't, it's just going to eat you up inside. We all make mistakes," she told him, trying to get him to forgive himself for what he'd done.

"Mistakes?" he hollered. "This was more than a simple mistake. This was adultery, I was unfaithful to you." He watched helplessly as Mariah's tears ran down her face. "Honey, please don't cry," he said, pulling her into his arms.

"Evan, we have to put this behind us, or else our marriage is doomed. I don't want to lose you, nor do I want to lose my sister again."

"Okay, I'll try, but I just don't understand how we can."

"Besides, this situation is perfect for Chandler. If they get marry, then his child would be part Clemmens. It would be as if you had been the sperm donor for his child."

"I guess that's one way to look at the situation. Have you thought if or what are we going to tell the child about this when they're older?"

She shook her head. "I'm not sure. I've never been in a situation like this one before. We'll talk to Whitney about it, but I think telling them the truth would be best. I need to call Lindsay."

"You're going to tell her about me being the baby's father?" he asked, shocked that she was going to tell her sister."

"No, I was just going to tell her about finding Whitney, not about the baby or the baby's father. I think that's Whitney responsibility to do."

He nodded, then Mariah called Casey's home.

"Hello?"

"Lindsay, this is Mariah."

"How are you doing?"

"I'm well. I have some exciting news to tell you."

"You're pregnant?" she asked teasingly, not at all expecting the answer she got.

Mariah choked, surprised by her sister's question. She hadn't planned to tell her about her baby yet, but she would find out soon anyway, so she went ahead and confirmed it. "Matter of fact I am, but that isn't why I'm calling."

Lindsay was confused to why her sister had confirmed her condition, then quickly changed the subject. "Congratulations. So, what's up?"

"You'll never believe who just left here."

"I haven't an idea. Who?" Why were they playing this guessing game? What Lindsay really wanted to know was more about her sister's pregnancy.

"Whitney."

She could only think of one Whitney. "Our sister, Whitney?"

"The one and the same."

Tears filled her eyes. "How did she find you?"

"Would you believe she met Evan a couple of months ago and she'd come here to talk to him? She didn't know about me until I came into the room," she replied nervously, trying not to let the cat out of the bag about Evan being the father of Whitney's baby.

Lindsay could hear the stress in her sister's voice. "Mariah, what aren't you telling me?"

"What do you mean?" she asked, scared she was going to say the wrong thing.

"You sound funny. Something's wrong, I can feel it."

"It's just so wonderful that I've found two of my sisters."

"Why did she come to see Evan?" Lindsay figured that must be what the problem was.

Mariah laughed. "It's a complicated story and I rather not talk about it on the phone."

"Is everything okay with you and Evan?"

"Yes. I need to talk to Whitney to see when the best time for her would be for three of us to get together."

"If you two come here, any time will work for me. Otherwise, I'll have to work around Austin's schedule, especially if I'm going to leave him with Casey."

"You need to get out of that house, so you two come here. I'll call you when I know something definite." They said goodbye, she hung up, then called Whitney.

"Hello?" Whitney answered phone without any enthusiasm in her voice.

"Whitney, it's Mariah."

"Well?" she asked, holding her breath, expecting her sister to tell her the worst.

"The three of us will somehow work through this situation. We're sisters and I want you in my life."

"I'm glad. Are we going to tell the child who their real father is? And if we do, at what age do we tell them?"

"We don't have to decide today."

"That's what Chandler said, but these are things I have to know."

"We'll talk this over and decide together. Are you going to marry Chandler?" Mariah asked shyly.

"Wouldn't that just make this whole situation more complicated?" she asked, her voice shaking.

"No, I don't," she said, thinking that she really did wanted Whitney to marry Chandler. "How do you figure that?"

"At any family parties, I would be there with Chandler, Evan would be there with you, and whenever we looked at each other, we'd all know what had happened between Evan and me."

"Even if you don't marry him, I would still invite you to family gatherings."

"If I wasn't married to Chandler, I wouldn't have to be there."

"Whitney, you have to forget the past with my husband and move on. I'm going to."

"I can't understand how you can say that," Whitney said to her.

"I'm not willing to lose either of you." Mariah's heart was filled with anguish at her sister's pain.

"Chandler said something to me that made a lot of sense. He said that since neither of us remembered our night together, we wouldn't have any memories to haunt us regarding that night."

"Sounds like a smart man."

"He seems nice," Whitney replied slowly.

"He's a good guy and all he wants is to marry you and make your baby his family."

Whitney thought for a second before she responded to her sister. "So, you wouldn't object to me marrying Evan's brother?"

"I think it would be wonderful." She paused for a few seconds. "Whitney, I was wondering about something."

"What is it?" she asked, almost afraid of what she was going to ask.

She really didn't have a right to ask her question since it wasn't any of her business, but Whitney was her sister and she had the right to know. "Did Chandler have a chance to talk to you about his problem?" she inquired, unsure if he had told Whitney about his condition or not.

Whitney smiled at her sister's concern. "Yes, I know he can't father any children."

"Does that make a difference to you?" she asked with uncertainty.

Whitney giggled a hysterical laugh. "If he can accept me being pregnant by his brother, I definitely can accept his sterility," she said nastily.

"Whitney, please don't do this to yourself. It's not good for the baby for you to be this upset. For the baby's sake, you have to let what happen with Evan go."

"I'll try," she said with some fervor.

"I've called Lindsay and she wants to see you."

Whitney wasn't ready to see her sister just yet as she was still trying to deal with this situation with Evan and Mariah. "Does it have to be today?" she asked tearfully.

"Well I guess not, but she's anxious to talk to you," Mariah replied disappointedly, as she wanted her family together again, but the way Whitney was dragging her feet, it may never happen.

"Did you tell her that I had sex with your husband and is pregnant with his child?"

"Of, course not!"

"We need to decide who we're going to tell about this."

"I think it would be best if we told her together, if we tell her at all. If we do, Evan's brothers will need to be told as well. Are you going to marry Chandler?"

"Mariah, I don't see that happening. He asked me just to be nice," she told her sister. She really did want to marry Chandler and not just because it would make life easier for her. There was something about him that seemed to draw her to him, but she wasn't sure what it was. His kiss had been out of this world, which left her with an excited feeling strumming throughout her body.

"It wouldn't hurt to think about it." Mariah was frustrated, wishing she could force Whitney to marry Chandler.

"I will, but don't get your hopes up."

Mariah didn't respond to her comment. "Let me know when you're ready to meet Lindsay. Good-bye."

Whitney hadn't seen Lindsay for twenty years and knew she shouldn't put off seeing her again just because she felt uncomfortable about her situation with Mariah and Evan. "Mariah, wait," she called out before her sister could hang up.

"What is it?"

"I'll come over tomorrow after lunch to see Lindsay."

"Come for lunch."

"Okay. I'll see you then."

"Thanks for doing this. I know it's hard, but Lindsay is family and wants to see you." Mariah hung up the phone with a smile, thinking that maybe everything would work out after all. She picked up the phone and redialed Casey's number.

After she and Lindsay made lunch plans for tomorrow, she went to find her husband, as they needed to talk about whom else, they were going to tell regarding Whitney and the father of her baby.

"Evan, I talked to Whitney just a while ago. She's coming over tomorrow for lunch and Lindsay is going to join us.

Evan pulled his wife into his arms. "I know how much this mean to you to have two of your sisters in your life again."

"We need to decide if we're going to tell Lindsay about you and Whitney or should we just keep it between the four of us?"

Evan expression turned to one of frustration. "Good question, but I don't have answer. What do you think?"

"Your brothers and Lindsay are going to want to know who the father of her baby is once they're aware she's pregnant. I'm sure this child will have some of your characteristics, so there's bound to be questions to why he looks like a Clemmens. Since Morgan and Casey know about Chandler's condition, we can't very well tell them that he's the father."

"I guess we better have a family meeting with Whitney and Chandler," Evan said, dreading talking to Whitney.

"Do you think Chandler should be included in this meeting?"

"Why shouldn't he?" he asked, confused to why she didn't want Chandler to be there.

"Whitney may not marry him," she informed her husband.

Evan looked at his wife in puzzlement. "Do you have anything against them getting married."

"Of course not. You know how I feel about your brother; he's part of my family. Do you have a problem with it?"

"No. I think it would be nice if they were to get married. It might make thing easier for Whitney if she had someone on her side."

Mariah looked hurt. "You don't think I'm on her side?"

"Honey, even though you're her sister, to her you're the other woman."

"Still I don't think Chandler needs to be included in our discussion."

"I just thought that since he knows who the father is, he could give us his perspective of the situation."

Mariah nodded. "I guess you're right. I hadn't thought of it that way."

Evan called Chandler to ask what he thought they should do, and he said he thought it would be best if the four of them discuss this together. They arranged to meet that night after dinner so they could thrash out the pros and cons of who to tell regarding the father of Whitney's baby. Then Mariah called Whitney to tell her to come over for a meeting, forgetting to tell her that Chandler was going to be there too.

Whitney was petrified to see her sister alone, so she called Chandler on his cell phone.

"Hello?"

"Chandler, this is Whitney O'Rourke."

Chandler smiled at the sound of her voice. "How are you doing?"

"I have a problem and was wondering if you could help me."

"What's the problem this time?" he asked in a teasing manner.

"Mariah just called and wants me to come over to discuss who we're going to tell about Evan and me."

"I know. Evan just called me."

"I don't want to go alone. Can you pick me up?"

"I can, but it is going to cost you."

Whitney was shocked by his comment. "What do you want?" she asked nervously.

"Your first born," he replied honestly.

"What? You think this situation is funny?" she cried, hurt that he could joke about this.

"Whitney, I asked you to marry me. I want your baby to be mine."

"Chandler, this isn't going to work." How she wished it had been Chandler that night in Tulsa instead of Evan.

"What isn't?" He held his breath, hoping she wasn't referring to them getting married.

"You and I getting married."

"It could if you'll let it." There had to be a way to talk her into saying yes to his proposal.

She didn't want to talk any more about his proposal. "Are you going to pick me up or not?"

He sighed, trying to think of a way to talk her into accepting his proposal. "Give me your address."

A few hours later, Chandler pulled into Whitney's apartment parking lot. He smiled when he saw her outside pacing as she waited for him. He stopped his car, and Whitney got in. "Hello Whitney."

"Hello. Thank you for picking me up," she said, refusing to look at him.

"I apologize for my earlier comment about wanting your first born," he said, his words were spoken softly.

She gazed over at him, giving him a weak smile. "No need. I overreacted."

They were quiet on the trip to Evan's place. When they arrived, Chandler helped Whitney out of the car, took hold of her hand, and they walked to the house together. He knocked on the door, then he opened the screened door, and they entered the house.

Mariah met them at the door. "Thanks for coming. Evan is in the kitchen fixing us some tea."

They met for over an hour before they came to the decision to tell the immediate family the truth about the father of Whitney's baby. Mariah and Whitney would tell

Lindsay tomorrow at lunch, while Evan and Chandler told Morgan and Casey.

The next day nervous about this meeting, Whitney showed up ten minutes early. She was unsure how she was going to be able to eat any lunch for worrying about what Lindsay would think about her being pregnant by their brother-in-law. When the doorbell rang, Whitney jumped and grabbed hold of Mariah's hand. "Mariah, I'm scared."

Mariah squeezed her sister's hand. "It's going to be okay. You wait here and I'll go let her in." She hurried to the door to let Lindsay in and when she opened the door, she saw that Lindsay had her hands full.

In one hand, she had Austin's carrier and in the other, a large diaper bag. Mariah reached out and took hold of the carrier, and as she looked at her sister, she was surprised to see she had the same glow she saw when she looked at herself in the mirror and bet her last dollar that Lindsay was pregnant too and that Casey was the father.

Mariah smiled at her. "Come on. Whitney is in the family room waiting."

When Whitney saw Lindsay, she ran to her and embraced her. "Lindsay, you beautiful. You have a special glow to you. Are your pregnant?" As soon as she asked it, she wished she hadn't.

Lindsay didn't know how to respond. She wanted to tell her sisters her news, but she couldn't since she hadn't even told Casey about the baby she was carrying in her womb. "I don't remember any of you, but your name was familiar when Casey mentioned it to me," Lindsay responded instead.

The other two sisters noticed she didn't answer Whitney's question about being pregnant and that she'd made a quick change in the conversation, but neither of them commented on it.

"That day they took me away from school, I was told that my entire family was dead, but I had a hard time believing it. It didn't make sense because I knew you and Mariah had been at school," Whitney told Lindsay.

The sisters sat down and visited, telling each other stories about their childhood and their adoptive parents. After lunch, the three women returned to the family room and Mariah decided it was time to drop their bombshell.

"Whitney and I are pregnant," Mariah told her sister.

Whitney waited for the question about who the father of her child was.

"How wonderful!" Lindsay exclaimed, but still didn't mention her condition.

Whitney leaned over and took hold of Lindsay's hand. "I have something important to tell you," she muttered apprehensively.

When no one spoke, Lindsay realized something was wrong. "What's going on?" she asked looking back and forth between her sisters. "What's wrong? Has someone died?"

"No, nothing that serious. I don't know how to tell you this, but Evan is the father of my baby." After the words were out of her mouth, she held her breath, waiting for Lindsay to condemn her.

"Mariah's Evan?" she asked with disbelief. "I don't understand," she said, looked over at Mariah, then back at Whitney.

"I met Evan in Tulsa a few months ago, we had too much to drink, and somehow ended in bed together, but neither of us remembered that part."

Lindsay looked back and forth between her sisters. "Are you sure Evan is the father?" she asked. She looked at Mariah and couldn't understand how she could be acting so calmly.

"Yes," Whitney answered, but refused to look at her sister.

Lindsay looked at Mariah again. "You're okay with this?" she asked, shocked by Whitney's confession.

"What would you suggest I do? Divorce my husband and disown my sister?" Mariah asked coldly.

"I guess not, but I don't know if I could handle it as calmly as you seem to be doing." Lindsay didn't know what else to say to her sisters.

"We've decided to put the incident behind us and not dwell on it. This is just a family thing, and we aren't going to tell anyone else who the father is."

Lindsay nodded. "I guess that's why Casey is with Evan and Chandler right now."

"Yes. We thought it would be better to tell the rest of you this way. Morgan is out of town and will be told when he returns."

Lindsay stayed until Austin became fussy, she fed him, then she took him home to put him to bed. After she put the baby down for his nap, she went to find Casey, finding him in the office doing some research.

"Casey, we need to talk."

He nodded, assuming she was referring to the family meeting regarding their siblings. "I was sure surprised when Evan told us his news."

"Casey, that's not what I want to talk about."

"It isn't?" he asked, shock that she didn't want to talk about Whitney and Evan.

"No." She took hold of his hand and pulled him to the couch.

Fear filled Casey. Did Lindsay want to break off their engagement? "Do you want to break up?" he croaked out his question. "Are you upset because of Whitney and Evan's relationship?"

Lindsay let go of his hand and pulled him into her arms. "No, of course not." She moved back from him and grabbed hold of his hand again. "I wanted to tell you that we're going to have a baby."

"No!" he exclaimed with alarm, hoping she was teasing, as he wasn't prepared for this to be happening to them just yet.

"Yes," she replied, afraid of his panic response. "I take it you aren't happy about this."

"No, it isn't that. I just wasn't expecting this. We only made love once without protection."

She smiled at him. "That's all it takes."

"Well I know that," he replied, his voice full of knowledge of that fact.

She was hurt by curt response. "Weren't you the one who told me that the men in your family are very fertile?"

He tightened his grip on her hand. "Well yes, but still, it's a surprise."

"I hope it's a good one."

"Of course, it's a good one. I guess my mind is still on my brother's news. Did you know Chandler asked Whitney to marry him?"

Surprise filled her face. "No, I didn't. Neither of my sisters mentioned that. Was he serious?"

"Yes, he was." Casey then told her about Chandler's medical condition.

"How sad. I guess in a way, Whitey's baby would be a blessing for Chandler. I think I'll call Mariah and ask her about it."

When Lindsay called her sister, Mariah confirmed what Casey had told her regarding Chandler's proposal but told her that Whitney hadn't given him an answer yet.

"How would you feel if they did get married?" When Mariah didn't respond, Lindsay decided she'd hung up on her. "Mariah, are you still there?"

"Yes, I was trying to find the right words to explain their situation. I think I would worry less about both if I knew they had someone in their life. Chandler has been hurt in the past by the woman he's dated when he's told them about his medical problem." Should she tell Lindsay about Chandler's secret?

When Mariah didn't continue, Lindsay decided to tell her she knew about it. "Casey told me about it."

"I think if they were to marry, this would be the perfect solution for both dilemmas, but Whitney doesn't see it that way. She's worried that by marrying Chandler, she'd be causing me more pain, but in fact it would be just the opposite."

"Maybe you should tell her that. We'll just have to wait and see what happens."

CHAPTER NINE

Lindsay was glad the plane trip was finally over, exhausted from trying to take care of two children under the age of two during the trip home. Casey was supposed to have gone with her to Oklahoma to pick up Nicole, but there had been a problem at his company, and he had to work at the last minute. Since Austin couldn't be away from her for any length of time, she had taken him with her. Then once she'd arrived at her in-laws, Nicole had latched onto her, refusing to leave her mother's side and had even sat on her lap when she nursed Austin.

It had been hard on Lindsay to explain to the Haggards about Casey and their pending wedding, as well as telling them about the baby she was expecting, but she shouldn't have worried. Matt and Helen Haggard were happy that she had found someone new, especially happy to hear she had found not one, but two of her three sisters.

Carrying Austin in his carrier and Nicole in her arms, she slowly walked off the plane. The diaper bag's strap fell off her shoulder and down her arm to the carrier and started banging against her leg as she walked. Once she was out of way of the other passengers, she set the carrier and diaper bag down onto the floor, then started searching for Casey. When she saw him walking towards her, she smiled and waved at him. She was so absorbed at seeing Casey that she didn't notice another man waving at her too. Both men walked towards her, but it was the stranger who reached her first.

The man stopped in front of her and suddenly grabbed hold of her arm. "Do you want to explain to me why you disappeared on me the way you did? I thought our night together meant something special to you. Why didn't you even leave me a note before you took off? I didn't know how to get in touch with you," he flew his questions at her, then he looked down at Nicole and Austin. "Why didn't you tell me you had children?" he asked, screaming this question at her. "You knew I had a child."

Lindsay roughly jerked her arm away from him. "Sir, you have me confused with someone else. You do look familiar to me, but I definitely haven't slept with you. If you don't leave me alone, I'll scream loud enough that the whole airport will hear me."

The stranger laughed. "That's a load of crap. You expect me to believe I have you confused with someone else," he hollered at her.

Casey grabbed hold of the man's arm, jerking the man around to face him, ready to do him harm, but was surprised to see it was his brother. "Morgan, what's going on here?" he demanded.

"Casey, this is a private matter and I expect you to mind your own business."

"Since Lindsay is my fiancée that makes this my business," he replied coldly.

"What? This is the woman you're going to marry?" Morgan turned back to Lindsay. "Then why did you sleep with me? Why did you tell me your name was Lesley?" He fired at her, not even giving her a chance to answer the first question before he asked another.

"Lesley? You've met Lesley?" She started crying as she seized hold of his arm in a tight grip. "Where did you see her?"

Morgan's expression showed his confusion. "What are you talking about?" he asked, pulling his arm away from her. "Are you crazy or something?" he asked, his eyes searching deeply into hers.

Casey touched his brother's arm. "Lindsay and Lesley are Mariah's twin sisters. The twins and their sister, Whitney, were separated from Mariah when she was nine years old. Lindsay and Whitney have just been be reunited with Mariah. Lesley hasn't been found, but apparently you've seen her."

"Why haven't I ever heard anything about Mariah having any sisters?" He was hurt that his family hadn't bothered to tell him about Mariah missing sisters.

"I guess none of us realized you didn't know?"

"When did you find out about Mariah's sisters?"

"Shortly after your wife's death. We were talking about loses and Mariah told Chandler and me about her sisters."

A hurt expression showed on his face. "I still don't know why she didn't tell me about them?"

"You were grieving for Traci and weren't in the state of mind to hear about her losing her sisters when she was a child. As time passed, I forgot about them and it wasn't until I met Lindsay on my trip home with Austin that I remembered Mariah's story."

"I still don't know why nobody mentioned that the woman taking care of Austin was Mariah's sister."

"I assumed you already knew. Otherwise, I would have told you at Alexandra's funeral. Why are you at the airport anyway?"

"I took Hailey down to Traci's parents so she could spend some time with her grandparents. I had just gotten off the plane when I noticed Lindsay. How long ago did Whitney come back into Mariah's life?"

"Recently. In fact, I haven't even met her yet."

"How did they meet?"

"Whitney met Evan during his business trip to Tulsa." Casey was unsure if he should be the one to tell Morgan about their relationship and the baby. "Morgan,

I don't know if I should be the one to tell you this, but," he looked at Lindsay and saw her nod. "Whitney is pregnant with Evan's baby."

"What? This is a joke, right?" he asked, looking back and forth between the couple. "You can't mean our Evan?"

"I'm afraid I do." Casey then went on to explain how the situation had come about, as well as about Chandler proposing to Whitney.

"I see. That's going an interesting relationship." He then turned to Lindsay. "I apologize for my temper and rude words."

"I understand, but please tell me how you know Lesley," she asked, as she couldn't wait another second to ask about her sister.

"You remember that bad snowstorm we had a couple of months ago that stranded Hailey and I in Columbia?" he asked Casey.

"Yes."

"Lesley was the woman who we stayed with that night." A smile covered his face at the memory of Lesley and the wonderful sex they'd had.

"You're kidding?" Casey knew how the night had ended for the two of them but hadn't ever said anything to Lindsay about it. Of course, now she knew that Morgan had slept with her sister. He was surprised that he and his brothers were all involved in some way with the four sisters.

"No, I'm not."

"Do you know where she was from?"

"She said she lived in St. Louis and that she was a nurse by day and a writer by night. She was in Columbia to attend a writers' convention, but I don't have any way to contact her."

"My sister is a writer?" Lindsay asked, tears filling her eyes. "Did she say what type of stories she wrote?"

"She said she wrote romance novels but hasn't had anything published yet. She mentioned her mother used to be a writer."

Lindsay let out a sob. "My mother was writer too? I can't believe this. What was Lesley's last name?"

"She told me her last name was Arrington, but I don't know if that was her maiden name, her pseudonym name, or what."

Lindsay repeated the name. "I can't swear to it, but that name does seem familiar."

Casey pulled out his cell phone and dialed Evan's number.

"Hello?" Mariah answered absentmindedly, wishing they could find Lesley.

"Mariah, this is Casey. You're just the lady I wanted to talk to."

"Oh, you are a smooth talker," she teased. "What's up?"

"Do you remember what your last name was before your adoption?"

Many different thoughts ran through her head, but she couldn't figure out why Casey was asking her this question? "It was Arrington. Why do you want to know?"

He smiled at her response. "Are you sitting down?"

"Just a minute." Since she was pregnant, she didn't want to take any chances, so she sat down in the nearby chair. "Okay I'm sitting, now tell me," she stated, holding her breath as she waited for the news.

"I'm at the airport to pick up Lindsay and we ran into Morgan. When he saw Lindsay, he assumed she was Lesley." Casey was expecting to hear Mariah say something, but all he heard was silence on the other end of the phone. "Mariah, are you still there?"

"Why would Morgan think she was Lesley?" she asked slowly, trying hard not to jump to any conclusions.

"You won't believe this, but Lesley was the woman he and Hailey stayed with when they were stranded during that March snowstorm."

Mariah gasped. "Let me talk to him."

Casey handed the phone to his brother. "She wants to talk to you."

"Hello."

"Morgan, why didn't you tell me you knew my sister?" Pain filled her at his thoughtless gesture.

"I didn't know she was your sister until just now," he informed her quickly.

"She looks exactly like Lindsey," she cried.

"Mariah, this is the first time Lindsey and I have met. With her being busy finishing her book and taking care of Austin, and with me busy with Hailey and my job; it's been too hectic for us to find the time to meet."

"Lindsay looks like I did when I was younger. How could you have missed it?" she asked, her teeth clinched tight in her anger.

"I'm sorry. I didn't know until today you had any sisters, let alone looking for them. I'm sorry I didn't detect the family resemblance."

"Do you know where she's living?"

"She said she lived in St. Louis." When Mariah didn't respond, he handed the phone back to Casey. "I can't talk to her." He felt bad for unintentionally hurting his sister-in-law who he loved as a sister.

"Mariah, it's me," Casey told her.

"What happened to Morgan?"

"I'm afraid he feels too bad to talk."

"Does he have Lesley's phone number?"

"No, but he does know that her mother used to be a writer."

"Our mother was a writer," she informed him.

"What was your mother's name?"

"Pam Arrington."

Casey turned to Lindsay. "Mariah says that your mother's name was Pam Arrington."

"Oh, my God," Lindsay muttered, her face suddenly turned pale, her eyes rolled back of her head, and then she fainted.

Casey quickly dropped his cell phone to grab her before she could hit the floor. Nicole started crying, and Casey had to attempt to comfort the child, while struggling to revive Lindsay. Morgan picked up the phone to let Mariah know what was happening, all three concerned as to why Lindsay had fainted.

Slowly Lindsay opened her eyes. "What happened?" she asked. She pulled Nicole into her arms to reassure her and she quickly quit crying as her mother held her tightly against her chest.

"You fainted when I mentioned your mother's name."

"I've read some of Pam Arrington's books," she told them

"So?" Casey asked, unsure the significance of what she was saying.

"Recent publications. That means our mother didn't die when we were kids."

"What is going on?" Mariah screamed over the phone at Morgan. "How is Lindsay?"

Morgan looked at Lindsay, then Casey. "Mariah, just a minute." He handed the phone to Lindsay. "Mariah wants to know what's going on and I don't know how to tell her."

Lindsay took the phone from Morgan. "Mariah, Pam Arrington didn't die when we were little."

"How do you know that?" she asked slowly, her eyes filling with tears.

How could she tell her sister that their mother may still be alive? "Mariah, I don't know how to tell you, but Pam Arrington was still publishing novels as of two years ago."

Mariah fought to control her pounding heart. "Are you sure of this?" she asked, as the tears ran down her cheeks. "Do you think she's still alive?" She held her breath, anticipating the worst.

"We won't know until we can check it out. My guess would be that she is since she's probably in her late forties or early fifties."

"We need to have a family meeting."

"I'll call you later and we make plans," she said, then the two sisters hung up.

* * *

For Lesley, the past three months had been horrible for her as she waited for Morgan to call. It wasn't until the end of the second month after the incident that she realized that she was going to have his baby, but she still couldn't believe it. So much for all that, monthly cycle safe sex crap she'd learned in school. How stupid could she be? She should have made sure they took the proper precautions that night.

Each day as soon as she stepped into her apartment, the first thing she did was to check her answering machine, but there wasn't ever anything from him. As the days passed, she became more and more depressed, angry with herself for what happen in Columbia with the attractive man.

She still had to tell her mother her news, but she was too frightened. It wasn't as if Pam Arrington gave a damn what happened in Lesley's life. Since the death of her sisters, her mother always seemed mad at her for some reason. Maybe it was because she hadn't died when the rest of her family had.

She didn't really remember her father or her sisters that well, but she still had the pictures of her sisters. Lesley thought back to the day she found out about her family. All she could recall was her sisters had been there the day she'd gone to the hospital to have her tonsils out but gone when she woke up later that day. Each day the pain of losing her sisters became easier, but she still missed them, especially Lindsay, her twin.

When she wandered into her mother's apartment, the place was quiet, but she was sure her mother was home. "Mom," she called.

"I'm in here," a drunken voice called back.

Lesley strolled into the kitchen, and saw her mother sitting at the table with an almost empty bottle of bourbon in front of her. When the last boyfriend moved out, instead of accepting he was gone, and moving on, Pam had started drinking heavily to drown her sorrows with liquor. When she looked at her mother's face, she could tell she'd been drinking for a while because she was already intoxicated. Maybe this wasn't a good time to tell her mother about the baby.

"What are you doing here?" Pam asked, slurring her words.

Lesley walked to the table and sat down next to her mother. Thinking it was best to get her news over with so she could go home, she took a deep breath and let it out. "Mom, I'm pregnant."

Pam brought her hand up and slapped Lesley's face hard. "You're a tramp. You've always been a disappointment to me. I should have kept one of your sisters instead of you."

Lesley jerked back from the force of the slap, dazed by her mother's slap and her cruel words. Was it just her mother's drunken mind talking or was there something else going on? "What do you mean by that statement?" she demanded loudly.

"When your father moved out on us, I got rid of your sisters," she garbled.

Lesley jumped up and captured her mother's shirt in her fists. "What do you mean you got rid of them?" Had her mother murdered her sisters? Tears of anguish ran down her cheeks as despair filled her at the thought of her mother killing her sisters.

Pam pulled away from her. "I told you, I got rid of them."

"Did you kill them?"

"Of course not. How was I going to raise four children on my own?"

Lesley didn't realize how cold and self-centered her mother was until this moment. "Wouldn't you have gotten child support?"

"Your father lost his job, so I gave your sisters to the government so they could take care of them." She knew she'd done the right thing years ago.

"I'm sure he would have found a new one. What about getting government assistance for us?"

"I have you know I do have some pride," she slurred again.

"Mom, do you know what happened to any of them?

"No, I never asked." She couldn't very well tell her that everyone thought that both parents had been killed.

"Lindsay was my twin, wasn't she?"

Her mother looked at her through her redden eyes. "How do you remember her?"

She wasn't going to tell her about the pictures and have her slap her again. "I just do." Lesley stood to leave but stopped as she watched her mother poured more liquor into her glass. All these years she thought her father and sisters were dead. Now she knew it was possible that they were still alive. Were they looking for her? Why hadn't her father ever come to check on them?

"Mom, why didn't Dad ever try to get in touch with us?"

"I told him there had been a fire and all four of you girls were killed," she said, then laughed an eerily sounding giggle.

"Mom, I need to go." Lesley had to get out of the house before she strangled her mother. When she got home, she went straight to the computer to start searching her family's names on the Internet. It was the first time since meeting Morgan that she hadn't checked the answering machine the second she entered the house. She went to the white pages' website, typed in her last name, then each of her sisters' first names, but there weren't any hits for them.

Then she entered Erik Arrington's name, and when his address popped on the screen, she practically jumped out of her chair, totally surprise to see he lived in Kansas City, just a four to five-hour trip away.

She sat there for several minutes, wondering if this could be her father. She had a good sob, then she wiped away her tears, she wrote down his address and phone number. Now that she had this information, she wasn't sure what she should do with it. She couldn't very well call him up and tell him that she was his daughter as there was always the off chance that this man wasn't her father, but some stranger. She would just have to go to Kansas City and meet him in person.

It was then that she decided to quit her job and transfer to Kansas City to be closer to Morgan, and possibly even her own father. She still needed to talk to Morgan but didn't know what she would say to him. Maybe she should wait until at least she was living in the same city as he was before she tried to tell him about the baby.

The next week was filled with her applying for a new job in Kansas City. Two days later, she had an interview at North Kansas City Hospital and was hired on the spot. Lesley rented a small house within walking distance from the hospital, returned to St. Louis gave notice to her job, and two weeks later, she was moving into her new apartment. Her mother hadn't ever allowed her to have pets while she was growing up, so the first thing she did after she was settled in her place, was to adopt a kitten from a shelter.

She planned to make a doctor appointment, but never made the call, making one excuse after another.

Then before she knew it, she was four months along and she couldn't put off seeing the doctor any longer, so she made an appointment with one of the doctors who had an office in the same hospital she worked at.

The doctor was an older man and she liked his friendly manner but became nervous when she saw his face get a stricken look on it while he was listening to her abdomen.

"Doctor, what's wrong?" she whispered. Thinking the worst, she wished she hadn't waited so long to see him.

His kind eyes looked up at her. "I don't want to alarm you, but I believe I hear two heart beats."

"What?" her voice choking with emotion as her eyes started watering.

"You may be having twins. Do twins run in your family?"

She laughed a nervous laugh. "Yes, I'm a twin."

"I'll need to schedule you for a sonogram to be sure." He put his hand on her arm. "How do you feel about this news?"

"I'm not sure."

"What about the father?"

Lesley didn't want to tell him the truth, but he would know it eventually. "I haven't seen him since . . ."

She wiped her tears away. "He doesn't know about my condition yet, but I'll tell him today."

"Do you want me to tell him for you?"

Lesley smiled at him. "Thank you, but no, I'll do it." She still had the phone number that Morgan had called that day. She'd planned every day to call him, but then she would get nervous and put it off for another day.

"I'll leave to let you get dressed." He wrote out a prescription for prenatal vitamins and handed it to her. "Make an appointment at the front desk for the sonogram and next month's visit."

"I will. Thank you, Doctor Rowe."

When she got home, she fixed herself some hot chocolate, sat down at the kitchen table, and took her cell phone out of her purse. She took a deep breath, and then dialed the number that Morgan had called that day from her phone four months ago.

She was disheartened when the answering machine came on. A man's voice was saying it was the Clemmens' residence and to leave a message, but she became flustered as she thought of what she was going to say, and quickly hung up the phone. Her spirit was crushed, and she felt like crying, as she'd hoped to get Morgan's number today. She knew that she was procrastinating by hanging up and would have to call back and leave a message. She took another deep breath, then redialed the number, this time leaving a message.

"Hello. My name is Lesley Arrington. I'm looking for Morgan Clemmens and this is the only number I had for him. It is very important that I speak with him. My phone number is 816-569-6819. Thank you." She hung up the phone, set in down on the table, and then stared at it expecting it to ring at any second.

She sat there for an hour waiting for it to ring, but it remained quiet. She wanted to throw the phone across the room, but she knew it wouldn't have done any good. She debated whether to call her mother, but she hadn't forgiven her yet for what she'd done to her and her sisters. Besides, as far as she knew, her mother didn't even know she'd moved away, and probably didn't even care.

CHAPTER TEN

Evan walked into the quiet house and began looking for his wife, but when he couldn't find Mariah, he began to worry. Where she could have gone? He went to the answering machine to check if she'd left him a message on it and saw that there were two messages. He pushed the button and waited for the messages to begin.

"Evan, my sonogram appointment got rescheduled to 3:30 today. I couldn't get hold of you in time, so I called Morgan and he's taking me. If you get home in time, please join me at the doctor's office. I love you," she said.

The second message was for Morgan, but since Evan wanted to get to the doctor in time to see the sonogram, he didn't stay to listen. He would have to tell his brother about the message when he saw him at the doctors.

* * *

Lesley was in a state of shock as she looked at the sonogram and saw two little babies, saddened that she didn't have anyone with to share her news. Not anyone who cared anyway. Her new co-workers at her new job were nice, but she hadn't gotten close to any of them and she still wasn't talking to her mother.

She'd just stepped out into the waiting room when she saw Morgan sitting in the waiting room. Her first thought was he was there for her, and her heart started throbbing against her chest as she tried to find the words to explain about the babies, but before she could move towards him, she heard the nurse call for Mrs. Clemmens. She looked over at the person sitting next to him, quickly realizing he was there with his wife.

She was furious that he had lied to her about not being married, then let out a sigh, thinking she'd probably had left her phone message at his home. She didn't look at the woman, as her eyes were too busy watching Morgan remove his arm from around the woman's shoulder as he stood.

Morgan happened to look over at her, and when she saw his eyes on her, she panicked and ran out the office. She could hear him calling her name, but she didn't stop. She was afraid he would stop her, so she ran to the door to the stairs, jerked it open, and commenced running down them as fast as she could. The pain in her side finally made her slow down, but she continued running the best she could. She constantly looked over her shoulder for any signs of Morgan, but she didn't see him.

When she reached her car in the four-level parking garage, a man was just getting out of the vehicle next to her, but she wasn't paying any attention to him, as her mind was still on Morgan. She had backed in, so the driver side of her car was next to the man's car. She had just unlocked her door when she felt a hand on her arm. She turned ready for a fight; her eyes filled with fear as she looked at the stranger.

He looked at her, surprised by her expression, then smiled. "Lesley, wait, I just want to talk to you," the stranger called.

Lesley panicked. She wasn't sure how this man knew her name, but she wasn't going to give him the chance to hurt her. She yanked her arm from his grip, kicked him in his shin, then pushed him back against his vehicle. She got into her car, slammed the door closed, locking it as fast as she could.

While the man was trying to regain his balance, she started the car, and quickly shifted into drive, pulling out of the parking space without even taking the time to buckle her seatbelt. Her heart throbbed loudly in her chest as she pulled out of the parking garage into the bright sunlight. Her house was just down the street, but since she was afraid, the man might be following her, she drove right pass it as the last thing she wanted was for him to know where she lived.

As she drove, she frequently looked in her rearview mirror, but because of all the traffic behind her; she couldn't tell if he was following her. She was frustrated when she had to stop at several stoplights as she tried to escape the area without him finding her.

A few minutes later, she heard a police siren. When she realized she'd been speeding and he was after her, she slowed down and pulled off the highway.

"May I see your driver's license and resignation?"

"I can explain," she said hurriedly. "I don't expect you not to give me a ticket, but a man grabbed me in the hospital parking lot. He startled me and I ran out of there as fast as possible."

"Really." The officer gave her a look of disbelief at her statement, but when he looked at her more closely; he could tell she'd been crying recently. "Do you want to come to the station and give a statement?"

She gave him a weak smile. "No. As I think more about the incident, I think I just over reacted. The man knew my name, so I don't think he meant me any harm."

"How would he know your name?"

"I'm a nurse at that hospital, so maybe I'd taken care of him or one of his family members."

"You've been crying, so the confrontation must have upset you."

"No, it wasn't that. I've had a trying morning."

"Such as?"

She knew it wasn't any of his business, but she felt as if she had to tell someone her news. "I received news today that I'm expecting twins."

The young officer wasn't sure if she was giving him a load of crap or not but decided he would investigate a little further. "I bet your husband will be excited with the news." As soon as he spoke, he saw her tear up. "What's wrong?"

"I'm not married. While I was at the doctor's office, I saw the man who's the father in there with his wife."

"Damn! That got to hurt."

"Yes."

"My name is Charlie Miller. Can I meet you somewhere and we can get acquainted?"

She gave him a weak smile. "Just give me my ticket."

"So, it that a no?"

"Are you sure you want to get involved with a pregnant woman?"

"Yes, besides I think you're beautiful."

"Thank you, but I need to tell the father of my babies about them before I get involve with anyone else."

"I'll give you my phone number. If or when you want to meet, give me a call."

"I will."

"I won't write you a ticket this time, but if I stop you again for speeding I will."

"Thanks." She watched him in her rearview mirror get back into his vehicle. She made sure her lane was clear, then pulled back onto the highway. When she saw the ramp off the highway, she took it, made a U-turn and started towards home.

* * *

"Lesley, wait," Morgan called after her.

Mariah grabbed hold of his arm. "You saw Lesley? My sister, Lesley?"

"She just ran out of here."

"Mrs. Clemmens," the nurse called again.

"Go after her," she told him.

"Mariah, I came here for you."

"I want you to go after her."

"Since she ran away, I take it that she doesn't want to have anything to do with me."

"Why was she here? Could she be pregnant?"

Morgan thought back to the night the two of them had made love. Since he hadn't used a condom and if Lesley hadn't been on the pill, there was a chance she could be pregnant with his child. "Yes, there's a good chance she could be."

"I see," she muttered, thinking that another sister pregnant by a Clemmens. Who would ever believe something like this could happen in one family?

The two walked towards the nurse and then followed her down the hall. Morgan waited outside the room while they got Mariah ready for the test, and then a nurse opened the door to let him in. Morgan kept his eyes off his sister-in-law's naked belly, looking at the monitor instead as he watched in awe his brother's child moving inside the womb, but Lesley wasn't forgotten.

* * *

At first, Evan was surprised to see Lindsay in the hospital parking lot, but when the terror in her eyes didn't dissipate as she stared at him, he instantly knew this couldn't be Lindsay. This woman had to be Mariah's twin sister, Lesley, the last missing one. "Lesley, wait, I just want to talk to you."

She yanked her arm from him, kicked him in his shin, then pushed him back against his vehicle and by the time Evan regain his balance, the woman was gone. "Damn," he banged his fist against his car. He looked down at his watch, saw the time, and knew he was late for Mariah's appointment; her sister would have to wait.

When he entered the office, he saw the room was filled with pregnant woman, each with a belly at different stages of the birthing process, but he didn't see Mariah or

Morgan. He went to the window to tell the receptionist who he was and inquire about Mariah.

The young woman smiled at him. "Your wife mentioned you may be showing up. I'll let someone know you're here."

Evan waited by the door and when it opened, he was surprised to see Morgan standing there. "Hey, brother."

Hailey was returning from her visit with her maternal grandparents today, and if Morgan didn't hurry, he would be late getting to the airport. "Go down to room three, they're waiting for you. I have to go because I have to go pick up Hailey at the airport. I'll see you all later."

"Thanks man." Evan started through the door but stopped suddenly as he remembered the message for Morgan at his place. "Morgan," he called after him.

"What?" He turned to look at Evan, anxious to go pick up his daughter.

"There is a phone message at my place for you. The lady said it was very important."

"Do you know who it was from?"

"I'm sorry, I don't know, I didn't stop to listen to it."

"Mr. Clemmens," a nurse called. "We're waiting for you."

"I got to go." Evan waved as he took off down the hall. When he entered the room, he saw Mariah lying on a table, and a technician was moving a probe across her stomach. He looked over at the monitor next to her and saw his child for the first time. The technician pointed to the baby's heart. Tears filled Evan's eyes as he watched the little pulsating heart on the monitor and in the excitement of the sonogram, he forgot to tell Mariah about seeing Lesley in the parking lot.

* * *

As Morgan drove to the airport, he thought about seeing Lesley at the doctor's office and wondered what it could mean. Woman went to see these types of doctors for other reasons too and just because he'd seen her there didn't mean that she was pregnant. Why was Lesley in Kansas City? Wouldn't she have gotten hold of him by now if she were in the family way? *Damn*! He slammed his fist on the steering wheel.

How was he going to find her and explain about Mariah? He arrived at the airport just as the plane he was to meet was unloading. After he picked up Hailey, said good-bye to his in-laws, he started for the parking lot, with Hailey telling him about her trip, and Lesley was forgotten.

It wasn't until Hailey had fallen asleep on the way home that he started thinking about Lesley. Remembering the phone message that Evan had mentioned, he decided to stop at their place before going home, as just maybe, the message would be from Lesley.

Mariah was surprised when she opened the door to see Morgan and Hailey standing on her front porch. "Morgan, what are you doing here?" she asked, giving him a worried look.

"Did you get a chance to listen to the message for me on your answering machine?"

"I wasn't aware there was one on it for you," Mariah responded to his question.

"May I come in?" He wasn't sure if she would have anything more to do with him now that she knew about his relationship with her sister.

"Of course," she replied, with a smile, moving back and let them in. He put Hailey down and she ran head of them into the living room. Mariah grabbed hold of Morgan's hand and gave it a tight squeeze. "We'll find her."

"If only I had already met Lindsay before my trip. Then I would have known who Lesley was when we met."

"Don't beat yourself up about it. I don't blame you," she said to reassured him.

They went into the living room and found Hailey sitting on Evan's lap telling him about her trip with her grandparents. Morgan went to the answering machine, pushed the button, and the messages began. The first one was Mariah's message, then the second one started.

"Hello. My name is Lesley Arrington. I'm looking for Morgan Clemmens and this is the only number I had for him. It is very important that I speak with him. My phone number is . . ."

In the excitement of hearing Lesley's voice, Hailey jumped off her uncle's lap and ran to the machine. When Morgan saw where she was going, he called out to stop her, but he wasn't in time. She pushed a button on the machine thinking it was the volume control, but instead of it getting louder, the message stopped.

He felt like screaming when he heard the machine click and quickly erasing the message. Morgan wanted to stomp and yell at his child, but he didn't, as he knew she hadn't done it on purpose. He looked at his brother for help.

"Do you have caller ID?"

"We haven't gotten around to buying new phones with that capability on them."

"Did you happen to have written the phone number down?"

"No, I'm sorry I didn't. When I heard Mariah's message, I was sort of sidetracked. So much has been going on here that I forgot to check the machine when we came home, so neither of us had even listened to it. I'm sure when you don't call her, she'll call back."

Morgan shook his head. "You don't understand. She saw me earlier in the doctor's office with Mariah, and I had my arm was around her shoulder when the nurse called out Mrs. Clemmens. She probably thought I was there with my wife." Morgan saw Evan's mouth dropped at his statement. "What's wrong?"

Evan turned to his wife. "Oh honey, I forgot to tell you, I saw Lesley in the parking lot when I was getting out of my car at the hospital today. I called out her name and put my hand on her arm, but she kicked me and got away."

"I don't understand. Why didn't you tell me you saw her?" Morgan asked, holding his breath as he waited for his brother's answer.

Evan looked strangely at his brother. "Why would you want to know about me seeing Mariah's sister?"

"I thought you knew Lesley was the woman I stayed with in Columbia."

"How was I to know they were the same person? I don't remember you mentioning her last name to me. Besides, when I saw the sonogram of my baby, I forgot all about even mentioning her to Mariah."

Mariah put her hand on Morgan's arm to calm him. "You saw her at the doctor's office. Maybe we can get them to give us her phone number," she excitedly told the two men.

Morgan shook his head. "You know they won't do that."

"Maybe they could get a message to her for us. If I explain the situation to them and tell them that she's my long-lost sister, maybe they could at least give us a number."

"Maybe twenty years ago they could, but now the Privacy Act prevents them from giving out that kind of information."

"It won't hurt to try," Mariah said, hopefully.

"Call them."

Mariah called her doctor's office, explaining the situation to the receptionist, saying all she wanted was to get a message to Lesley Arrington, who was a patient of one of the doctors.

When the receptionist said she would do her best to get a message to Lesley, Mariah thanked her and hung up. The woman called Lesley's number and left Mariah's message, but as soon as the message finished, her new kitten walked across the answering machine, erasing the message. As Lesley had done when she'd left the message for Morgan, the three Clemmens sat there, waiting for the phone to ring.

CHAPTER ELEVEN

Lesley was asleep, dreaming about Morgan when the phone rang, she reached out in the darkness for the phone. "Hello?" she answered groggily.

"Miss Arrington? Lesley Arrington?" a man asked.

"Yes, this is Lesley Arrington."

"This is Sam Johnson at St. Louis University Hospital."

The mention of the hospital made Lesley jerk up in bed. "Is it my mother?"

"Yes. I'm sorry to tell you this, but she passed away a few minutes ago."

"What happened?"

"She had been drinking at a local bar, then got into her car, ran off the road, and crashed into a tree."

"Was anyone else hurt?" Lesley asked, a sick feeling of dread filled her.

"No, just your mother."

She was relieved to hear that at least. "That's good to know."

"Do you want us to make funeral arrangements for you?"

"You can do that?" she asked, relieved that she wouldn't have to take care of that for her mother.

"Yes."

"It would probably be easier for you to do it from there. Would you mind?"

"Do you have a preference of her burial?"

"She wanted to be cremated. There isn't any family left but me, so there isn't any need for a service."

"I'll call you later when everything has been finalized."

"Thank you so much for calling and letting me know about my mother. I'll need to arrange for time off at my job, and then I'll be down."

She gave the man her cell number, and then hung up the phone. She felt she should have cried when she heard the news about her mother, but her hatred for what she'd done to her and her sisters prevented her from feeling sad about her death.

She called the HR department at work, leaving a message to explain about her mother's death and that she wouldn't be in for the rest of the week. She quickly packed a suitcase, then went into the kitchen to make sure the kitten had enough food and water to last her until she could return home.

Lesley headed out for her trip to St. Louis and depending on traffic and the number of times she stopped, the trip would take her five hours. When she arrived in Columbia, she stopped to eat a late breakfast and to stretch her legs. When she reached St. Louis, she went straight to the funeral home to take care of her mother's cremation. She bought a plot for mother's ashes, then went to a restaurant for lunch. She wanted to order an alcoholic drink to calm her nerves, but because of the babies, she didn't.

After lunch, she drove to a public storage facility to buy boxes, then she drove to her mother's apartment to begin cleaning it out. She opened the door and stepped inside. As she looked around the only home she remembered, she began to cry.

After she had a good cry, she took some trash bags and began piling her mother's clothes into them. Then she started packing the rest of her mother's belongings into boxes. She had originally thought she would dispose of everything, but then decided that someday when she didn't hate her mother as much as she did right now, she might want some of her personal items.

There was an empty beer bottle on the living room floor, and because she was so angry with her mother, she kicked the bottle with her foot, then watched it spin underneath the couch. Now she was angry with herself for her actions.

She walked over to the couch and knelt to retrieve the bottle. Her hand reached under the couch, but instead of feeling the bottle, she felt a smooth, flat object. She pulled it out and looked down at it, surprised to see a picture of her and Lindsay, covered with many years of dust. She quickly sat down of the floor, letting her tears fall as she looked at the picture she had lost so long ago. After she had a good cry, she stood to finish want she was here to do.

She took the clothes to a nearby thrift store, then returned to the apartment for the rest of her mother's belongings and packed her car. She was sitting on the couch, trying to decide what to with the furniture, when someone knocked at the door. When she opened it, Martin Webber, her old classmate, who lived in the building was standing there. "Hello, Martin."

"I heard on the news about your mother. I'm sorry about her death."

"Thank you. Do you want to come in?"

"Thanks, but I can't stay."

Lesley noticed that Martin seemed a bit nervous. "Martin, is something wrong?"

"No," he replied slowly, as if he wanted to say something more.

"What is it?" Her eyes watched him as he struggled with what he wanted to say.

"I have a question to ask," he said, staring down at his feet, refusing to look her in the eye.

"Martin, please tell me. What is it?"

Martin looked up at her. "I don't know how to ask it."

"We've known each other for a long time, just ask."

"Can I have some of your mother's furniture?" he asked just above a whisper.

She reached out for his hand. "Martin that would help me greatly. Take anything you want."

Martin smiled. "Really? You sure you don't want any of it?"

"I live in Kansas City now. I don't have the room for any of this stuff. Anything you take is less for me to have to deal with."

"Can I have all of it?" he asked slowly, afraid she would think he was being too greedy.

"Why would you want it all?" Lesley was surprised by his question, as she had been thinking he might want the couch or maybe the bed, never dreaming he would want everything.

"Cindy Adams and I are going to be married," he quickly added.

"Congratulations," she told him, squeezing his hand.

"I do have one more favor to ask."

"What's that?" Since he was already getting all the furniture, Lesley couldn't think of what that favor could be.

"Can we have your mother's apartment?" His eyes watched hers, waiting for her anger.

Of all the things he could have asked, this question had floored her. "I guess so," she replied, a bit stunned by his request.

"I'm sorry. I shouldn't have asked that. It's just we can't get married until we find a place to live. This place is perfect since it's close to my parents and our jobs."

"Let's go talk to the landlord. If he doesn't mind, then you can have the place today."

Martin leaned over and kissed cheek. "Thank you."

Lesley was relieved the way everything had worked out today. Now all she had to do was go home and call Morgan to tell him about the baby, but good luck didn't stay with her for her return home. A mile out of town a drunk driver rammed into her car, causing her car to run off the road and slam into the concrete barrier. She was rushed by ambulance to the hospital and monitored overnight to make sure the babies were okay. She was released the next day, and since her car had been totaled, she took a taxi to the airport and got a seat on the last flight to Kansas City, having all her belongings shipped home.

* * *

Casey was returning home from Oklahoma, but because of a severe thunderstorm just out of Little Rock, his flight had arrived in Kansas City thirty minutes late. Lindsay had been upset with him leaving town since their wedding rehearsal was scheduled for tonight, but his sister's house had sold, and he'd gone there to sign the contract on it. He was supposed to meet her and her sisters at the church at six and it was almost that now. He figured he'd better call to tell her that he was going to be late; he had just pulled out his cell phone when he happened to glance up to see Lindsay ahead of him. When he didn't see either of the children with her, he figured she had left them with Mariah.

"Lindsay," he called out, but she didn't respond. He was puzzled why she hadn't turned when he'd called out her name, then realized that she hadn't heard him over all the noise in the airport as she continued to walk away from him. He didn't want her to get out of his sight and started to run after her. He saw her stop at another baggage claim, but before he could reach her, she picked up a suitcase off the carousel and started walking away. He was confused to why she was taking someone's luggage with her.

"Lindsay," he called again, but this time louder. Still she didn't acknowledge him. Casey started running faster to meet up with her. "Lindsay," he said as he gripped hold of her arm and turned her towards him. "Didn't you hear me calling you?"

"Excuse me?" the woman asked, frightened by the stranger's rough treatment of her.

"Why are you here? Where's Austin?"

"Take your hands off me," she demanded.

"Are you still mad at me about leaving on this trip?" He didn't think she would be, but who knew how a pregnant woman would act half the time.

"I'm sorry, but you have me confused with someone else. I've never seen you before in my life. My name is . . ."

Before she could finish her sentence, he interrupted her. "You're Lesley!" he replied excitedly, grabbing hold of both her arms.

She looked at him with surprise. "How do you know my name?" she asked, pulling away from him. Was this man some sort of stalker? As she studied him, she became aware that he reminded her of the man from the hospital parking lot and even a bit like Morgan.

He reached to the back of his pants, pulled out his billfold, and opened it up to show her the picture he had of Lindsay, Nicole, Austin, and himself. "I'm engaged to . . ." he stopped and smiled at her, "your twin sister," he said.

"You know my sister?" she asked tearfully, while looking at the picture in his hand.

"Yes. Your three sisters have been looking for you for the last few months."

"You know all three of them?" she asked tearfully.

"They are all living here in the Kansas City area."

The tears began falling down Lesley's cheek. "Growing up, I didn't know what had happened to them. It wasn't until recently that I found out that they hadn't died as I had been told when I was a child."

"Lindsay didn't remember that she even had sisters until she met Mariah's husband a few months ago and Whitney had been told that all of you were dead. Do you live here in town?"

"I do now. I had been living in St Louis until just recently." She looked down at the picture in her hand and then back at him. "Are these your children?"

"The baby is my nephew and the little girl is Lindsay's daughter from her first marriage."

"She's divorced?" she asked, hoping that was the case.

"No, her husband died."

"How awful. The last time I saw Lindsey, we were only five years old."

"I'm sorry I didn't introduce myself, I'm Casey Pennay. Lindsay and I are getting married this weekend, and I'm already late for my wedding rehearsal."

"Congratulations. You better get going, I would hate to make you to be any later."

"Come with me and surprise the family."

"I can't crash your party," she cried.

"Don't think of it that way. Consider it as making it the happiest day in Lindsay's life." He took hold of her hand. "It will be the happiest day in all three of your sisters' life. Please come with me," he begged, grabbing hold of her hand.

Lesley jumped in surprise when Casey seized hold of her hand. "Thank you, but I need to take care of some personal business first. Maybe I could just come to the wedding tomorrow."

"Actually, the wedding isn't for another four days. Tonight, was the only night this week we could all get together for the rehearsal. If I don't bring you with me tonight, your sisters will be angry with me. One thing I have learned recently about your twin sister is that you don't want to make her angry."

Lesley laughed. "I guess I could make my phone call from here and then I'll be able to join you."

"I'll go get my luggage while you make your phone call. Did your park your car here?"

"No. While I was in St. Louis, I was in an accident and my car was totaled. So, I decided to fly home and buy a new car here."

"Is someone coming to pick you up?"

"No, I was going to take a taxi home."

"I'll meet you back here and then I'll take you to see your sisters."

Lesley smiled at him. "I can hardly wait."

Casey waved as he hurried away, dialing his cell phone as he returned to claim his luggage.

"Hello?"

"Lindsay, I'm sorry, but my flight was running late and I'm just now picking up my luggage. I hope you aren't mad at me."

"You can't control the airlines," she replied, hiding her anxiety from him

"I know, but I still feel bad for being late. To make up for it, I'm bringing you a surprise."

She smiled at his comment. "Honey, you don't have to do that."

"This is one surprise you're going to love; I guarantee it."

"Okay. I'll see you when you get here."

CHAPTER TWELVE

Morgan and Hailey were to pick up Evan and Mariah for the rehearsal, but he had a flat tire on the way and now was running late. When he arrived, he and Hailey hurried to the door and knocked.

Mariah let them in. "We're going to be late," she grumbled at him.

"I'm sorry. I didn't plan on getting a flat tire," he replied sharply.

Mariah clutched his hand. "Morgan, please accept my apology. I'm just a bit edgy tonight."

"What is it? Is it the baby?" His eyes looked down at her.

"No, I just feel something bad is about to happen." She gave him an edgy look.

"Nothing bad is going to happen." He gave her hand a quick squeeze.

"I wish we could have found Lesley, then this celebration would have been more special," she cried.

Morgan took her into his arms and gave her a tight hug. "We'll find her."

"Morgan, you are going to have to get yourself your own wife," Evan whispered behind his brother's ear.

Morgan laughed as he moved away from Mariah. "As soon as I can find someone like yours, I will," he sighed, thinking of Lesley.

The phone rang and Mariah jumped. "It's bad news," she cried. "I just know it. If you had been on time, we would have already been gone," she shouted at her brother-in-law. "This call is going to be something bad."

It rang a second time before Evan reached for it as the other two just stared at it.

"Hello?"

"Is this the Clemmens residence?"

"Yes, it is."

"I need to get a message to Morgan Clemmens, and this is the only number I have for him. May I leave a message with you?"

"Just a minute," he replied, smiling at his nervous wife, and then handed the phone to his brother. "Someone wants to talk to you," he said, smiling happily at him, figuring this was Lesley calling back.

Morgan assumed it was one of his brothers. "Hello?" he answered, looking at Evan and Mariah as he waited for someone to speak to him. "Is someone there?"

"I need to leave a message for Morgan," she said, unsure if this new voice was Morgan or not.

Since it had been a month since Lesley had called, he hadn't expected to hear a familiar woman's voice, but he was too afraid to hope, thinking the voice might belong to Lindsay. "This is Morgan. Who is this?" he asked, wanting to make sure it wasn't Lindsay before jumping to any conclusions.

"Lesley Arrington," she stated.

"Lesley, please don't hang up. Let me explain about the other day."

"There's no need to explain. Since you saw me in the doctor's office, I assume you know I'm pregnant. I just wanted you to know that I'm expecting twins and you're the father. I don't want you to leave your wife nor am I asking for any money," she quickly rambled.

"Oh, my God! Lesley, you must listen to me. The woman you saw me with is my sister-in-law, not my wife. She's married to my brother Evan. Lesley, we have to meet so we can talk."

"I can't today. I've been invited to my twin sister's wedding rehearsal, then I'm going to dinner with them. I'm at the airport with her fiancé and he's taking me to the church."

"You're with Casey?" Morgan couldn't believe this was happening. Soon, they would be together again.

"You know him too?"

Morgan laughed. "You could say that. Casey is my younger brother," he told her. He waited for a few seconds, but she didn't respond back to him. "Lesley, are you still there?"

"He told me his last name was Pennay and you said yours was Clemmens. One of you has lied to me," she said angrily.

Morgan had to restrain from laughing at her comment. "I swear no one has lied to you. He and I had different fathers. Casey and our younger sister were from our mother's second marriage."

"I see," she replied, not really believing him.

"Ask him if you don't believe me, he'll tell you."

"I will," she said, her words cold and sharp.

"You go on with Casey. Hailey and I are driving Mariah and Evan to the church, we'll meet you there. By the way, Evan was the man who grabbed you in the parking lot at the hospital that day?"

"Why did he do that? I don't understand. How did he know my name?"

"He's married to your sister, Mariah."

"What?" she cried. "Are you sure?" Her hand tightened on the phone as she waited for his response.

He smiled to himself. "Yes, I'm sure. My brother, Chandler, and your sister, Whitney will be joining us at the church."

"My mother told me why we were torn apart like we were."

"Wait, are you saying you have spoken to your mother?" Morgan was stunned by her information.

"Yes, but . . . ," she started, but Morgan interrupted before she could tell him her mother was dead.

"Hold on a minute," he said.

Lesley could hear him telling someone what she'd just said.

"Hello? Lesley, this is Mariah," she said, smiling to herself before she continued, "your sister. Tell me what you just told Morgan."

"Our mother gave you, Whitney and Lindsay away because our father left her."

"No!" Mariah cried.

Lesley told her everything she knew concerning their mother abandoning them and her recent death. "When I found out that our father could still be alive, I looked him up on the Internet.

"Is he still alive?" Mariah was almost too afraid to hope.

"If he's the man I found, he is. I haven't tried to contact him yet, so I don't know if he's our father."

"Where does he live?"

"He lives here in Kansas City, but I want to hear about our sisters."

"Would you believe Whitney and I are both pregnant?" Mariah laughed.

"Really? Who's Whitney married to?"

Mariah was quiet for a few seconds. How could she explain it to her sister she hadn't seen for twenty years that her husband was the father of Whitney's baby? "Whitney isn't married."

Lesley laughed. "Well it's good to know I'm not going to the only unwed mother in the family."

"So, you are expecting?"

"Yes," she replied, but didn't tell Mariah that Morgan was the father. "I'm going to have twins."

"How exciting! Congratulations. You must be thrilled."

"I should be, but it's going to be hard being a single mother with two babies."

"Well anything can happen between now and when the babies come. Maybe you and Morgan will get together."

By her comment, Lesley knew that her sister was aware he was the father of her babies. "Maybe," she said, not commenting either way.

"We better hang up and get going to the church. We'll talk more when we get there, otherwise Lindsay will have a fit if we're all late."

"I'll see you soon. Bye, Mariah."

"Bye, Lesley," she said, smiling at the thought of finally being reunited with the last missing sister.

Lesley disconnection and heard someone call her name, she looked up to see Casey walking towards her and she waved.

"Let me carry your bag for you."

"Thank you. I just talked to my sister, Mariah. I hear we're already related through her and her husband," she said, then waited for him to tell her that Morgan was his brother.

"Yes, Evan and Mariah have been married for several years."

"I should tell you that I know Morgan and his daughter."

Casey smiled a knowing grin at her. "I know."

Lesley blushed. "I take it that you know how we met."

"Yes, I'm aware of the sleep over."

"Did he have to tell everyone?" she asked angrily, embarrassed this man knew they had slept together.

"Wait a minute," he said, putting his hand on her arm to calm her. "It wasn't like that. A few weeks ago, Morgan ran into Lindsay at the airport and naturally, he assumed she was you. He accidentally let the cat out of the bag when he was talking to her."

"Oh." She felt embarrassed for her sharp tone. "I'm sorry for my outburst."

"Morgan is a gentleman. I don't think he told anyone anything that he shouldn't have."

She decided it would be best to change the topic of their conversation. "Tell me about Lindsay."

Casey smiled at her delicate tactic of changing the subject of their conversation. He started out by telling her about Lindsay's husband, Bryon and their daughter, and then he told her about Bryon's death. He parked the car, got out and hurried around to help Lesley out of the car. "Leave your suitcase here for now."

"Okay. Do I look all right?" she asked nervously.

"You look fine, but your sisters aren't going to care how you look."

They stepped into the church and Casey looked around for any sign of his family, but when he didn't see anyone, he went to the room where the reception was going to be held. Before he entered, he told Lesley to wait outside until he called for her, then he stepped into the room.

"Casey, you made it. Mariah and her group are running late too. I expect they should be here any minute," she said, giving him a warm smile. "I've missed you."

Casey gave her a quick kiss, then looked around for Whitney and Chandler, but he didn't see either of them anywhere. "Am I the first one here?"

"Whitney's in the ladies' room."

"Where's Chandler?"

"He's probably outside the door waiting for Whitney."

Casey laughed. "The love bug sure has bitten him hard." When he saw Lindsay looking at his hands, he smiled, knowing she was looking for his surprise. "What are you looking for?"

"Where's my surprise?"

"Close your eyes," he said teasingly.

"Come on," she said, with a small pout, "I'm too old to do that."

"Close your eyes," he insisted, "or you won't get the surprise." While she closed her eyes, he hurried to the door, opened it, and motioned Lesley in. "Come in and stand here," he whispered, then he turned back to Lindsay. "Okay, you can open them now."

Lindsay opened her eyes and looked right at her sister. "Oh, my God!" she cried. "I can't believe it," she muttered through her tears, then she ran to Lesley and threw her arms around her. "A few months ago, I didn't even remember having any sisters. Now I've been reunited with all of them." She turned to Casey. "Thank you."

"I really didn't do anything except to run into her at the airport."

Lindsay looked at her sister. "Thank you for taking sure good care of Morgan and Hailey."

"I didn't do that much," she said, and then blushed.

Lindsay didn't comment on her redden cheeks. "According to Hailey, you save their lives."

Lesley laughed. "I wouldn't go that far."

"Lesley," a woman called with longing behind her.

She looked towards the voice and saw a woman who was an older version of herself. "Mariah?" she asked tearfully.

"Yes." Mariah hurried to her sister and hugged her tightly to her. "I didn't think I'd ever see any of you again. Now here we are all together."

"We have so much to talk about," Lesley said to her sisters

"Yes, we do."

"I have some pictures at my place of us when we were little."

"I can't wait to see them. The only one I have is that last one of the four of us. Why didn't you ever call me?"

"Mom told me you were all dead. It wasn't until recently that I knew you all could still be alive, but I didn't know where you were living."

"I'm talking about when you got my message that day Morgan saw you at the doctors' office."

Lesley frowned at her. "What message?"

"The receptionist at the doctors' office was going to leave you a message to call me."

"If she did, I didn't get it. I have a new kitten at home who likes to walk on the table where my answering machine is. She must have stepped on it and erased the message."

"Lesley," a familiar male voice called.

Lesley moved away from Mariah in time to have child run into her legs, then she looked up to see Morgan staring at her. "Hello, Morgan."

"We need to talk."

Lesley turned back to Morgan. "Yes, but I don't think this is the place to do it."

"No, but I have to tell you that I'm sorry about all that's happened."

She gave him a weak smile. "It takes two to tango. I'm as much to blame for thinking I was in a safe part of my cycle."

"Lesley, do you remember me?" Hailey asked, tugging on her dress to get her attention.

"Of course, I do." She knelt to eye level with the child. "I've missed you. What have you been doing?"

"I'm going to be in a wedding," she said, excitedly to Lesley.

"Are you going to be the flower girl?"

"Yes, and after the wedding I will have a new aunt and cousin."

"How exciting," she said, smiling at the child.

Hailey leaned closer to Lesley's ear. "I rather have a new mommy and a sister instead."

Hailey's words went straight to Lesley's heart. "I tell you what," she whispered back to the child.

"What?" she inquired excitedly; her eyes wide with anticipation.

"You're going to get part of your wish and I'll do my best to give you the other part."

"Which part am I going to get?" she asked animatedly.

Lesley laughed. "You'll just have to wait and see. Your daddy and I need to talk first."

Hailey grabbed Lesley's hand. "Go do it now," she screeched.

Lesley laughed, then stood up. "I think it should be later when your daddy and I are alone."

"Oh," Hailey replied disappointedly.

"As soon as Whitney and Chandler return, we'll get started on the rehearsal," Lindsay said to the group.

Lesley turned back to Lindsay. "Where have they gone?"

"Whitney was feeling a little under the weather."

CHAPTER THIRTEEN

Whitney felt better now that she'd thrown up, but she didn't know how she was going to survive this evening without being sick again. She wanted to be here for Lindsay, so she washed her face and dried it, then opened the bathroom door, but stopped quickly when she practically ran into Chandler. "What you are doing here?" she asked angrily.

"Waiting for you." His eyes looked over her, checking her color. "Are you okay?"

"You shouldn't be here," she told him hatefully.

"I wanted to make sure you were all right."

"It's not your responsibility," she yelled at him as she stomped passed him.

"Someone should care when you're sick," he answered back, his hand itching to grab hold of her.

Whitney felt awful for her hateful comment to him and turned around to face him. "I'm sorry for my rudeness. Thank you for caring." She turned to walk away, but a firm hand on her arm stopped her. She turned to look at Chandler, immediately seeing he was about to say something else to her. "Chandler, my answer is still no. I'm not going to marry you," she replied. She felt bad when she saw his miserable expression. "I'm sorry, but this whole situation with Evan and Mariah has me upset. I'm not comfortable being here and seeing the two of them together considering that I had sex with my sister's husband."

"Whitney, if you are going to have any kind of relationship with Mariah, you're going to have to forget about that night," he said tenderly.

"How in the Hell am I going to do that when I'm pregnant with Evan's baby," she shrieked just above a whisper at him, then broke into tears.

Chandler pulled her into his arms to comfort her. "Whitney, please say you'll marry me."

"Chandler, I think that would only make matters worse," she muttered against his chest. She didn't want to move away from the comfort of his arms, but knew she had to, so she gently moved her hands up and pushed away from him.

"I don't see how," he stated, grasping hold of one of her hands.

"If we were to marry, we would always be part of Evan and Mariah's family. If I was to marry someone outside the family, I wouldn't have to see Evan as much."

"He is your baby's father. I'm sure he'll want to be part of your baby's life."

That thought caused terror to run through her. "I don't know, we haven't talked about that yet."

"Hey, you two," Casey called to them. "It's time."

"I'm coming." Whitney pulled her hand free and hurried after Casey. When she walked into the room, she instantly saw her twin sisters standing side by side together. "Oh, my God!" she cried.

Lesley looked up just as Whitney joined them, and the two women embraced. "Whitney, it's so good to see you."

"Lesley, I would know you anywhere," Whitney told her sister.

"Really? You remember me?" Lesley was thrilled.

Whitney laughed. "Of course, I do, but I'd forgotten just how much the two of you look alike," she said breathlessly.

Lindsay clapped her hands. "Everyone," she called out to get everyone's attention. "It's time to get this rehearsal over with so that we can go to dinner."

Everyone followed her into the church to take their places and the rehearsal began. As soon as it was over, everyone started for the door of the church to go to their cars. Lesley started following Casey since she had ridden to the church with him.

"Lesley, why don't you ride to the restaurant with me?" Morgan called to her.

"Won't your car be too crowded? I thought Mariah and Evan were riding with you."

"No, they aren't."

"Then how are they getting to the restaurant?" she asked, looking around for Mariah.

"They're driving Whitney's car for her and they're taking Hailey with them to give us a chance to talk."

She was afraid to be alone with him, but she knew that eventually they would have to talk. "Then I guess I'll ride with you." Morgan took hold of her arm and they headed towards his car. "Is Whitney still feeling under the weather?"

"Yes. I can empathize with her and her nausea," he said, thinking of when his wife had been expecting Hailey.

Lesley giggled at his comment. "And you know this from experience?" she joked.

Morgan's expression turned grim before he responded. "Yes."

Lesley looked at his heartbreaking expression, suddenly realizing he must be referring to his wife. "I'm sorry for my comment, I wasn't thinking."

"Have you been bothered with morning sickness?" he asked just as they arrived at his car,

"No, not at all."

He helped her into the vehicle, then started his car and pulled out into the street before he spoke again. "Traci, my wife, had morning sickness worse than most women, but I think Whitney's morning sickness is due more because she's upset being pregnant by a married man and who that man is, than anything else."

"Whitney told me who the father of her baby was. I think she was afraid I would disown her because of it. I told her about us and that I was pregnant with twins. It seemed to make her feel a bit better."

"I glad to hear you're telling your family about us," he uttered, then looked over at her.

"I think some of them knew before I told them. Would you know anything about that?" she asked, closely watching his expression.

"I'm not going to lie to you. Mariah and Evan knew about the baby only because I'd saw you at the doctor's office that day. Lindsay and Casey found out that we'd been intimate when I ran into your sister at the airport, thinking she was you."

"That's what Casey told me. Do you think Whitney will marry your brother?" she asked, trying to move the conversation from them.

"I have my doubts."

"Why's that? Isn't Chandler good husband material?"

"Well," he started, but didn't know if he should tell her about his brother's condition or not.

"You're not sure?"

"Chandler has a medical condition that may make a difference to someone planning a life with him."

Lesley grabbed hold of his arm. "He isn't dying, is he," she inquired softly, tears threatening to fall at the thought of him dying.

Morgan reached down and patted her hand. "No, it isn't that serious. He can live a full life, but he can't ever father any children."

"Oh, I didn't know."

"Whitney does, but I don't think that's what preventing her from accepting his proposal."

"You think it's because of Evan and Mariah?"

"Yes, but enough about our family. What are you and I going to do about our situation?"

Lesley wanted to ask him how he felt about her but couldn't find the nerve to ask. "I want you and Hailey to be in the babies' life. Other than that, I'm not sure what we should do," she replied timidly.

"This really isn't the time or place to talk about all this, but I would like to see us married before you have the babies."

Lesley tried to keep her elation from showing at his words as she looked over at him, trying to find her tongue to say something to him when he glanced over at her.

"You don't want that?" he asked uncertainly, afraid she wouldn't marry him.

"No, I would like that," she replied shyly, then slightly blushed.

"Are you sure?" His eyes flashed over at her, then quickly returned to the road.

She turned her head away and looked out the windshield. "I don't know how to explain my feelings."

"Please try." He gave her a quick look, then returned his attention to his driving.

It was now or never. "I do have very strong feelings for you, otherwise I would have never gone to bed with you, and I would love to be Hailey's mother."

Morgan quickly pulled the car over to the side of the road and put the car into park. "Does that mean you'll marry me?"

"Yes, it does," she said, giving him a shy smile.

"How are we going to tell Hailey about all this?"

"Maybe after dinner, we can sit her down and explain that we are going to get married and in five months she's going to be the big sister to two babies."

"I know my daughter well, she's going to ask when we're getting married."

Lesley grinned at him. "Then we better have an answer for her," she replied, thinking next week would work for her.

"I don't want to rush you, but I think we should get married as soon as possible."

Lesley didn't want him to feel obligated to marry her. "Morgan, I don't want to force you into marrying me."

Morgan took hold of her hand. "Is that what you think you're doing?" When she nodded, he continued speaking. "Lesley, maybe we are rushing things a bit, but I think that we have something special between us. Maybe we wouldn't be planning to get married as soon as we are if it weren't for the babies, but I think even if you weren't pregnant, we would still have ended up getting married."

She looked up and gave him a weak smile. "You really think so?"

"I know how I feel about you and I haven't felt that way since Teri died."

His words brought a warm glow to her heart. "Okay. We'll plan the wedding to be soon."

"Should we seal the deal with a kiss?"

Lesley laughed. "I don't think so," she uttered, thinking where his last kiss had taken them.

He gave her a hurt look, wondering why she didn't want him to kiss her. "Why not?"

"Then we would never get to the restaurant," she teased, her eyes twinkling with amusement.

"Damn! We better get going or we're going to get in trouble with that sister of yours."

Lesley laughed. "To think you know my sister better than I do."

"She's a wonderful person, all your sisters are."

The family was waiting for them when they arrived, then the group was seated in a private room. As they waited for their dinner to arrive, the four sisters talked about their lives, but once the food arrived, the room became quiet, as everyone was busy eating. When the dinner dishes were gone, and everyone was eating their desserts, Casey and Lindsay stood up.

"Lindsay and I want to thank everyone for being here this evening. The last few months have been filled with many surprises, some good, some not so good," he said as he looked around the room. "The biggest surprise being the four Arrington sisters finding each other after a twenty years separation. Of course, we can't forget about Nicole, who will become my daughter tomorrow. We survived the loss of Alexandra and Clayton, Austin moving in with us, and all the babies on their way to join our family later this year." Casey stopped to look at Lindsay, he saw her smiled and nodded her head.

"Just so we won't be left out of this baby boom this family is having, I want to tell you that we're going to have a baby in November too."

Loud screams were heard throughout the room and Lindsay's sisters moved to congratulate the new mother-to-be, and Casey's three brothers patted him on the back, passing on their good wishes.

As the others moved away to finish their desserts, Morgan stepped over to speak with Casey. "I need to talk to you privately for a few moments."

Casey was concerned that something was wrong. "Sure. Let's step outside to talk."

The two men left the others and went outside so they could talk in private.

"Okay, what's up?" Casey asked, expecting the worst.

"How would you and Lindsay feel if Lesley and I shared your special day with the two of you on Sunday?"

Casey grinned at his brother. "So, I take it she said yes to your proposal."

Morgan nodded. "She did."

"Congratulations," he said, patting him on the back. "I'm sure Lindsay wouldn't mind, but maybe we should ask her first."

Morgan agreed and the two men returned to the others. Casey went directly to Lindsay, pulling her away from Mariah and Whitney, leaving Nicole and Austin with their aunts to watch over them.

"Casey, what's wrong?" she asked him, worried that he had some bad news to tell her.

"There isn't anything wrong. I just wanted to ask if you mind sharing our wedding with Morgan and Lesley."

Lindsay let out a scream of exhilaration, and Casey quickly covered her mouth with his hand. "I take that as a yes." He laughed when she nodded behind his hand. "Do you want me to tell Morgan?"

She pulled his hand away and held on to it. "We'll do it together."

The couple returned inside, then moved to where Morgan and a nervous Lesley were standing watching them.

"Well?" Morgan asked, unsure by Lindsay's expression what their decision had been. He looked over at his brother, when Casey gave him a wink, he let out the breath he'd been holding.

Lindsay reached out and took hold of Lesley's hand. "Casey and I would be honored to share our day with you."

Lesley leaned over and gave her sister a big hug. "Thank you."

"Shall we tell the others?" Casey asked to two women.

Lindsay giggled. "No, let's surprise them."

The foursome agreed and the two couples moved away to mingle with the rest of the family. When the party broke up, Casey and Lindsay took the children home so that they could put the little ones to bed. Chandler offered to drive Whitney home, but she told him she was feeling well enough to drive. Evan asked if Chandler could take them home, and he agreed, wishing he were with Whitney instead. Morgan, Hailey, and Lesley were the last to leave. When they arrived at Lesley's place, he helped Hailey out of the car, then helped Lesley out.

"Where are we?" Hailey asked as she looked at the small house in front of her.

"This is where Lesley lives."

They went into the house, then Morgan sat down, and called Hailey to him. When she stood beside him, he pulled her onto his lap as Lesley sat down next to him.

"Hailey, on Sunday when Uncle Casey marries Lindsay, there's going to be an additional wedding."

Hailey looked over at Lesley, then back to her father. "Who?"

"Lesley and I are going to be married too."

Hailey screamed, throwing her arms around her father as she looked over at Lesley and smiled.

"Sweetheart, we have another surprise to tell you."

Hailey couldn't imagine what it could be. "What is it?"

Just then, the kitten jumped on to Hailey's lap.

"I'm going to get a kitten too," she said excitedly.

Lesley smiled. "Tabby can be your kitten, but that isn't what the other surprise is."

"Lesley is going to have two babies," Morgan told her.

"At once?" Hailey asked, her eyes wide in awe.

"Yes, and you will be their big sister," Morgan informed her.

Hailey looked back at Lesley. "You don't have to do that. I just wanted one."

Lesley laughed. "Sometimes nature has a mind of its own. Since Lindsay and I are twins, I guess I was more likely to have twins."

"Are they going to be brothers or sisters?"

"That's going to be a surprise," her father replied.

"I want to know now," she whined.

"I think we better leave so I can get this young lady home and into bed."

Lesley reached over and took hold of Hailey's hand. "Your father and I don't know yet, but as soon as we do, we'll let you know. Okay?"

Hailey smiled. "Okay."

Morgan stood with Hailey in his arms, then he leaned over and gave Lesley a quick kiss. "We need to get our marriage license tomorrow. I'll call you tomorrow when we get up."

CHAPTER FOURTEEN

Before Lindsay was ready for it, her wedding day arrived, and it was going to be even more special for her than she had first imagined. Not only were her three sisters in her life again, but her twin sister was at her side sharing her wedding with her.

The twins met at the church, and when Mariah and Whitney entered the room, they were surprised to see Lesley getting dressed in a wedding dress as well. Lesley told them that she was wearing their mother's wedding dress, then told them the story of why her mother had done what she did to them. The other three sisters began to cry, after a few minutes, they dried their tears and decided not to dwell on it but go on with their lives as if they'd never been apart.

Hailey walked down the aisle first, throwing rose petals as she walked to where Casey and Morgan stood waiting. She stopped next to her father, then turned to watch the brides. Evan walked Lindsay to Casey, then Chandler and Lesley followed behind them. Each was kissed by their escort, and then handed to their grooms. Lindsay and Casey were married first, then Lesley and

Morgan. After their vows were spoken, and the minister pronounced them husbands and wives, told them they could kiss, then the two couples walked down the aisle hand in hand.

They had a buffet dinner, then after everyone had eaten, they cut the cake. There was dancing and the four brothers took turns dancing with each of the four sisters and it was late when the party finally broke up. Casey and Lindsay returned home with the children, planning to take a honeymoon after Austin was weaned so that they could leave him with family. Morgan, Lesley, and Hailey were spending the weekend at the Great Wolf Lodge, an indoor water park in Kansas City, Kansas, which wasn't far from their house.

* * *

Erik Arrington stared at the picture in the paper of the two brides. The caption under the picture read Lindsay Haggard and Lesley Arrington were married in a double wedding ceremony. The article said Lindsay had married Casey Pennay and Lesley had married Morgan Clemmens, and the two men were half-brothers. The story went on to say the two brides had recently been reunited with each other as well as with their two older sisters, Whitney O'Rourke and Mariah Clemmens, after a twenty-year separation. The article mentioned that

Mariah was married to Evan, Casey and Morgan's oldest brother.

The four girls in the article were his daughters, all these years he thought they were dead. Why had Pam lied to him? He remembered her phone call as if it was yesterday. The memory was still very painful for him and didn't realize he was crying until he felt a drop of moisture hit his hand.

He had moved to Kansas City to find a job, but before he could find one, Pam called to tell him their marriage was over. When he told her, he wanted to see his daughters, she told him there had been a terrible fire and all four of the girls had been killed. He mentioned that he would come home for the funeral, but Pam told him not to bother because she had had them cremated and thrown their ashes to the wind.

Erik grabbed the phone book, opened it and started flipping through it until he found Casey Pennay's number, and then quickly dialed it.

"Hello?" a female voice answered.

"Is this Lindsay Pennay?" he asked nervously.

"Yes," she replied, smiling at the sound of her new name.

"Your sisters are Mariah, Whitney, and Lesley?"

"Who is this?" Lindsay asked, afraid some nut that had seen their picture in the paper, calling to cause trouble for her.

"Erik Arrington," he said, "your father," he quickly added.

"How did you find me?" she asked tearfully, barely able to ask her question.

"I saw yours and Lesley's wedding photo in the paper."

"Why did you desert us?" she yelled at him, as Lesley hadn't told her the lie her mother had told their father.

"Your mother told me you were all dead. How was I to know she lied? What happened after I left? Why was there a twenty-year separation between all of you?"

Lindsay quickly explained to him what her mother had done to the four sisters. Telling him that three of them had been put up for adoption, but for some reason she had kept Lesley with her.

Erik asked about Pam, and Lindsay told him she had died recently. She went on to tell him that all four of them were expecting babies in November, and that Lesley was having twins. She told him that she had a daughter from a previous marriage, and her husband's nephew was living with them. They talk for a few minutes more, then Erik told her that he wanted to see them, and they made plans to meet. As soon as they hung up, Lindsay called her sisters and told them she had a special surprise for them.

* * *

The next evening Chandler called to ask Whitney out for a date, she pleasantly thanked him, but told him no. She had just hung up the phone, her hand still on it, when it rang again. She jumped back, putting her hand on her chest, as she tried to calm her pounding heart as she picked it up. "Hello?" she squawked.

"Whitney, this is Lindsay. Are you okay? You sound funny."

"I had been talking to Chandler and had just hung up, when the phone rang, it surprised me is all."

"I'm sorry."

"No problem. What's up?"

"I need for you to come to our house."

"When do you want me?" she asked, thinking she would say sometime later today.

"Now!"

"Now? What is so urgent that it can't wait?" Whitney couldn't think of any reason she would want her at her house so quickly.

"I can't say," Lindsay replied secretly.

"Why do you need me?" Panic filled her. "Does this have anything to do with Chandler?"

"No. I have a surprise and I need for the four of us together when I show it."

"Can you at least give me some sort of hint?"

"This is a very big surprise," Lindsay told her.

"That all you're going to say?"

"I can't take the chance of giving the surprise away."

"All right I'll be there as soon as I can."

* * *

Lindsay called the other two sisters, asking them and their husband to come over as well. It wasn't long before she heard the knock at the door and hurried to answer it. When she opened the door, she was surprised to see a tall older man standing there, a man who resembled her and her sisters.

"Hello," the man said to her.

"I don't need to ask who you are," she said, pushing the screen door open. "Please come in."

"Is it all right if I hug you?" he asked, his eyes closely watching her.

"Yes," she responded, her eyes filling with tears.

Erik gave Lindsay a quick hug. "I can't believe this is happening. All these years I thought all of you were dead and now you are back in my life."

Lindsay moved away from him. "I want to introduce you to my husband."

"It's nice to meet you," Casey said, putting his hand out to Erik. "I'm Casey Pennay."

"Erik Arrington, it's nice to meet you."

"The rest of the family will be here shortly," Lindsay told her father. "Why don't we wait in the living room for them."

"Where are your daughter and nephew?" Erik asked, looking around the room for the children.

"They're both taking a nap, but Nicole should be waking up shortly."

The doorbell rang.

"Why don't you and I go check on Nicole? We'll stay out of sight until the whole family has gathered," Casey told the older man.

Soon Lindsey's sisters were assembled in her home, with the men in their lives standing nearby. Casey rejoined Lindsay with Nicole in his arms, she smiled at him before she stepped in front of the group.

"If everyone will face this way, I'll present my big surprise." Her family turned towards her. "May I introduce to you," she started, then turned toward the door. "A man who thought we were all dead, Mr. Erik Arrington, our father."

When Erik stepped into the room, several screams were heard as he was quickly engulfed by his other three daughter. Soon everyone was talking at once, with tears in their eyes.

* * *

The next day, Chandler call again to ask if Whitney would go out with him, and again, she told him no. Then he called her again the day after that, and she refused again, but that didn't deter him as he called her every day for the rest of that week.

Friday night just as Whitney opened the door to her studio apartment, she heard her phone ringing, but before she could answer it, it quit. She was tired from her day at work and all she wanted to do was take off her dress, laid down, and rest. She pulled her couch out to a bed and had just removed her dress when the phone rang again, then she sat down on the bed to answer the phone. "Hello?"

"Guess who?" Chandler teased.

"Chandler, why do you keep calling me?" She couldn't take much more of this.

"You know why, and I'm not going to stop until you agree to go out with me at least once."

"I think it's sweet you want to take care of me, but I'm not your concern," she muttered.

"You're family, so that makes you my concern."

"Maybe so, but that doesn't mean we have to get married."

"You want to live in sin with me," he teased.

"Chandler," she cried, her voice choking on her tears.

He instantly felt bad for his bad humor when he realized he had hurt her feelings. "I'm sorry. That was a crude joke, but I am serious about marrying you."

"Maybe it wouldn't hurt for us to get together without our families breathing down our back to talk, but I can't guarantee anything."

"A date is a good start. Is tonight too soon for you?" he asked hurriedly.

She turned and looked longingly at the bed behind her. "I guess not."

"I'll be there in ten minutes," he said, then he hung up the phone before she could stop him.

Whitney just sat there in a daze for a few seconds with the phone still to her ear before she realized she had better get redressed, otherwise he would showed up at her door and find her in her bra and underwear and with her bed looking inviting in the background.

She looked over at the clock and wondered how long it would be before she could go to bed, for that's what she really wanted to do. Even though she was expecting him, she still jumped when Chandler knocked at the door. She hurried to the door and opened it.

"Well, don't you clean up nicely," she teased, since the last time she'd seen him; he had been wearing a tuxedo. When he didn't respond to her joke, she wondered what could be wrong. "Is something wrong?"

"You're beautiful," he said with admiration. "Pregnancy becomes you."

His comment made her uncomfortable. "I'm ready to go." She stepped outside and quickly shut the door before he could see into her tiny apartment as the last thing she wanted was for him to see her bed sitting in the middle of the living room since she didn't see any reason to return the bed back into a couch.

He smiled at her, assuming she was in a hurry because she was anxious to go out with him. "I hope you like *54th Bar & Grill*."

"Yes, I do. It's one of my favorite places to eat," she replied honestly.

They were quiet during the trip to the restaurant as neither one of them were sure what to talk about. When they arrived, the hostess sat them, she handed them their menus, then left. Whitney opened the menu even though she knew what she was going to order as she felt uneasy sitting across from Chandler, unsure what to say to him.

"Do you have room in your place for the baby?"

She laughed at the thought of the baby in her tiny apartment. "Hardly, I live in a studio apartment."

"Not much room to add a husband and a baby."

"I don't need room for a husband because I'm not getting married."

"We need to start looking for a house before we get married, don't you think?" he asked, pretending he hadn't heard what she had just said.

She laughed. "You don't give up do you?"

"No. If you marry me, you can quit your job and stay home to take care of the little one. My apartment is bigger than yours, so we could move in it after we're married, but before the baby comes, I would like to buy a house."

"Let's talk about something else." She didn't tell him that she didn't need a house, as she wasn't going to marry this man. He did do funny things to her equilibrium, but still he was a stranger to her.

When Chandler took her home, he walked her to the front door, then watched as she unlocked her apartment door. When he saw her opened it just enough for her to pass through, he realized she was going to move inside without letting him kiss her, and he swiftly grabbed hold of her wrist. "I want to kiss you good night."

She quickly pulled away from him. "Chandler, this just isn't going to work."

"I want to take care of you." His eyes became teary. "I want your child to be mine."

She put her hand on his arm. "I know you do, but I think it would be best if we just stay friends, instead of getting married."

He moved his arm away from her wrist, moving it around her waist as fast as a striking snake. "I want to be a father and I want that child to be yours," he muttered, then brought his lips to hers. The kiss continued as he slowly moved them into the apartment, swiftly closing the door behind him.

Chandler moved her backward until they encountered something that blocked their movement, then he quickly opened his eyes to see what had stopped them and was surprised to see the bed. He was aware that studio apartments were very small, and that the living room and the bedroom were the same, but he hadn't been expecting the bed to be pulled out. He pushed her down on to the bed, his lips never leaving hers as he began unbuttoning her dress. He kept expecting Whitney to stop him, but she never did. As quickly as possible, he undressed her, and when she was naked, he undressed himself, joined her on the bed and then he made them one.

Afterwards as they laid there in her bed, Whitney tried to feel guilty for what she had let happen between them, but she couldn't. She couldn't fight all the feelings she for this man any longer. If he still wanted to marry her and be her baby's father, then she would say yes, the next time he asked. She felt a movement next to her and turned to face him, smiling when she saw his expression of wonderment. "Are you okay?"

"Never in my life have I experience anything as marvelous at that was."

She laughed. "Now that's a bunch of bull if I ever heard any."

Chandler turned and pulled her to him. "I swear it isn't. I think we have something special between us." He kissed her. "Just a moment," he said softly to her, then moved away and leaned over the bed to grab his pants. He put his hand into the pocket and pulled out a small box.

Whitney's heart practically stopped when she saw the box in his hand. Could it contain a ring? She was afraid to hope as her eyes returned to his face.

Chandler opened the box and pulled out a diamond ring. "If you don't like it, we can exchange it, but when I saw it, I thought of you."

All she could do was nod as her tears made words impossible. It was the most beautiful ring she'd ever seen; it had a small diamond in the middle, surrounded with several smaller sapphires.

"Will you marry me?"

"Chandler, are you sure?" She looked deep into his eyes as she waited for his response.

"Yes, I'm sure."

"Then yes, I'll marry you."

Chandler gently took her hand and put the ring on her finger. "Now we need to seal it with a kiss."

Whitney giggled. "If I do, we'll probably never leave this bed."

He grinned at her. "I would like to test out your theory."

It wasn't until the next morning before either one of them did leave the bed for good. Chandler told her that he had to go home to change clothes, then he would be back to take her to breakfast. As soon as he left, Whitney went to take her shower. An hour later Chandler was knocking at her door, Whitney opened it and invited him in.

"Whitney, I want to give this to you," he said, then handed her a check.

She took the check from him, then swore when she saw it was written for one hundred thousand dollars and that it is made out to her. "What is this for?" She didn't understand why he was giving her this check. Certainly, it couldn't be for they had done together in her bed last night.

"I want you to buy us a place that is big enough for the three of us to live."

She let out a loud sigh, relieved by his answer. "Isn't this a little big for a down payment?"

"You don't have to put it all down on the house. You could save some of the money to make repairs to the house if necessary. You know, such as new carpet and fresh paint. Whatever you want."

"Shouldn't we find a place together?" She was hurt that he expected her to find a place on her own.

"We should, but I'm really busy at work and can't take the time to go house shopping with you right now. I hope you understand." He felt bad, asking her to find them a home without him, but if they waited until he has some spare time, it might be another month or so.

"What if I find a place and you don't like it?"

Chandler took hold of her hand. "As long as we are together, I don't care what you buy. Just tell me when and where, and I'll be there to sign the paperwork on it. Now let's go to breakfast."

CHAPTER FIFTEEN

After breakfast, Chandler returned her to her apartment, then left to tend to some business at work. Whitney called Jack Billings, a realtor, explaining to him what she was looking for. Three days later, Jack called to tell Whitney that he had the perfect place for her, saying that it was a great bargain because the owner had passed away and the family was anxious to get rid of it. They set up a time to go look at the house for the next afternoon.

When Jack stopped by Whitney's apartment the next day, he was instantly attracted to her, but when he saw the engagement ring on her finger, he knew she wasn't available. They talked nonstop on the way to the house, but when they pulled up into the driveway and saw the sight that greeted them, they were both speechless.

The yard was filled with twelve old vehicles in several stages of disrepair, the house had peeling paint on the two sides they could see, and the front porch looked as if it would blow down with the next gust of wind.

"I'm sorry Miss O'Rourke. I hadn't any idea the place looked this bad. I guess I should have figured there was a reason they were asking such a ridiculous low price for the place."

"Maybe the house isn't as bad as it looks," she added hopefully.

"I wouldn't bet on it," he commented sarcastically.

They got out of the car and maneuvered their way around the cars to the front porch. Whitney didn't know much about cars, but she did know enough to realize these vehicles were very old models and that someone would probably pay good money to get their hands on these vintage cars. Her mind was busy thinking about how she could go about getting rid of them and make a profit at the same time.

They carefully stepped onto the front porch. Jack pulled open the wooden screen door, jumping back when it fell off in his hands. He laid the door against the house; unlock the front door and they slowly entered the house.

Whitney's eyes swiftly inspected the first room, seeing that the wallpaper was a disgrace, and the wooden floor had all sort of scratches and scuffmarks covering it, but that didn't discourage her to the house's potential.

With a good refurbishment, the walls and the floors would be as good as new. As they walked through the house, Whitney became more excited and knew that this property wouldn't last long once a person with the right vision saw it. The house had three bedrooms, a living room, a dining room, and a kitchen with a washer and dryer hookup in it.

"There's a barn out back. Do you want to look at it?"

"Might as well since we're here," she muttered, afraid it wouldn't be useable. If so, she wasn't sure if she wanted this place.

They stepped out the back door, and from where they stood, they could see the old barn, and Whitney was surprise how good it looked from where she stood.

"I wonder how it looks inside."

"Only one way to find out," he said, carefully stepping down the steps.

They didn't speak as they walked down the brick walkway to the barn. Jack grabbed the door handle and pulled the door back, it let out a loud squeak as he slid the door along its track, then they slowly stepped into the barn. Right smack in the middle of the barn was another old car. This one was considerably older but was unquestionably in better shape than the vehicles in the yard. As Whitney's eyes moved away from the car, she saw the five horse stalls along one wall. The barn was in excellent shape, needing only a good cleaning and a fresh coat of paint, then it would be perfect to use for horses.

"Jack, I want it."

He turned to her, his mouth dropping open from his shock. "You got to be kidding. This place is a worthless mess."

"No, with a good restoration on the house, a good cleaning everywhere else, this place will be great."

"Are you sure?" He wanted to talk her out of this, but a sale was a sale.

"Yes. It's exactly what I want."

"Don't you want to talk to your fiancé before you make a decision?"

"No, Chandler told he didn't care what I bought, and this is the place I want."

"I'll start on the paperwork for an offer as soon as I get back to the office. Do you want to offer less than they're asking?" he asked hopefully.

"No." She didn't want there to be any reasons the seller would refuse to sell her the property.

He hated to see her waste her money for this run-down place. "You should," he said, thinking how he hated the thought of this lovely woman buying this place at this price, especially in its dilapidated condition. "How much do you want to put down?"

"I'll give you a fifty-thousand-dollar deposit."

"That much?"

"I don't want to take the chance someone else could steal the place out from under from me."

"I doubt that's likely to happen," he said as they returned to the house.

She smiled at him. "You just don't have the imagination to envision what this place will look like after the right repairs. Give me six weeks and you won't recognize the place."

"Maybe I should give you six months just to be sure."

Whitney laughed. "Let's bet on it."

He nodded. "Okay, what kind of bet?" He would like to take her to bed, but he doubted she would go for that kind of bet.

"Whoever loses takes the winner out to lunch."

He put out his hand. "It's a bet."

When they got back to her apartment, they said their good-byes and Jack promised to call her as soon as he knew if the seller accepted her offer or not. Whitney called Chandler, excitedly telling him that she had found the house she wanted to buy. He told her that he would like to see it before he signed anything, but that was the last thing she wanted. She knew he would try to talk her out of buying the property if he saw the horrible condition of the place, so she begged him to let her fix it up before he saw it, and he promised he would.

An hour later, Jack called Whitney to tell her that she'd just bought a house and the paperwork was ready for signing. Whitney left work to meet Chandler at the realtor's office, telling her boss that she would be gone for the rest of the day. Chandler looked at the price of the house on the contract and was satisfied with it. He just was glad Whitney had found a place, and now they could set the date to get married, so he didn't read over the description of the property, so he wasn't aware that a barn and eighty acres came with the house. After he signed his share of the mountain-size amount of paperwork on their new house, he turned to Whitney. "Well, I guess we now own a house."

"When can I start working on it?" she asked excitedly.

"As soon as I give you the keys to it," he teased.

"Can I have them today?" she asked sexually, giving him an inviting grin.

He laughed, then handed her a set of keys, but then quickly pulled them back.

Whitney quickly looked up at him. "What's wrong?" she muttered nervously; afraid he'd change his mind about seeing the house.

"I want a kiss first."

She let out a sigh of relief. "No problem."

He gave her a swift kiss, then handed her the keys. "Here you go."

"Thank you," she responded absentmindedly as she was already thinking about all the remodeling projects she wanted to have done on the house before he could see the place.

He laughed, knowing where her mind was. "I can't wait to see this place."

She quickly glanced at him. "Now Chandler you promised you wouldn't look at it until I'm ready for you to see it."

"How much work do you think it needs?" He was eager to see the place they were going to call home.

"Well," she hedged, "at least a week," she said, figuring she could keep putting him off until the house was completely done.

"Then we can set the wedding for a week from today?"

"Chandler, I . . ." she started as her mind went into turbo speed, trying to think of some logical reason to stall him, but wasn't sure what it could it be.

"I know a week isn't long enough for you to plan our wedding, but I'm sure with your sisters' help it could be done."

"Could I have two weeks instead?" she asked, thinking they would just have to live in his place until the house was ready.

"Two weeks and not a day longer," he teased, as his eyes bored into hers.

"Then two weeks it'll be." She grinned at him, wishing she didn't have to lie to him. "Thanks."

"You're welcome, I think."

She laughed at his comment. "I need to talk to Mariah."

He smiled at her. "You want to tell her all about our new house?"

She had to get his mind off that subject, so she used the best subject to do just that. "No, silly I want to talk to her about our wedding."

"Tell her not to go to overboard with the plans. I would like something small like the twins' wedding was."

She smiled at his comment. "I'll follow you to the office so that I can talk to her today," she said as they walked out of the realtor's office together.

"I have a meeting to go to when I get back to the office, so I'll just see you later." He leaned over and gave her a short kiss. "Think about quitting your job and being a full-time mother."

Her eyes watered up. "Oh, Chandler, I love the idea of being able to stay home with the baby. I'll give notice as soon as we have a definite date for the wedding."

They said good-bye before getting into their vehicles and heading in the direction of Clemmens Manufacturing. When Whitney arrived, she hurried into the office, telling the receptionist that she needed to see Mariah. Soon she was sitting next to her sister; still feeling uncomfortable around her, tears appeared in her eyes as she thought of what she and Evan had done together.

Mariah frowned. "Whitney, do you have some bad news to tell me?"

Whitney grinned at her sister. "I wouldn't call it bad news."

"Then why the tears?"

"I was just thinking about us," she said, taking hold of her sister's hand.

Mariah wasn't fooled, she knew Whitney had been thinking about her relationship with Evan. "Whitney, you have to forget about that night with Evan."

"I'm trying, but I was thinking about the four of us being together again," she said, telling her sister a small white lie.

"Who would believe the way we found each other," Mariah said, smiling a warm grin, letting Whitney think she believed her lie. "Or how we are all related to one another with three of the husbands being brothers. I wish you'd marry Chandler, then all four of us would be married to brothers," she replied despondently.

"Well, if you're willing to help me plan the wedding, your wish will come true."

Mariah screamed, jumped up, and grabbed hold of her sister. "You said yes?"

"I did," she said breathlessly as Mariah gave her a tight hug.

Mariah stepped back from her sister. "You're not doing this just to make me happy are you?" Her eyes watched her closely as she waited for her response.

"No, Chandler and I decided this is what we both want."

"I hope it goes well for you."

"Me too," she said, giving her sister a weak smile.

"Let me get in touch with the twins, then I'll call you. How soon do you want the wedding?"

"We just bought a house."

Mariah screamed again. "How wonderful!"

"It needs a lot of work before we can move in, but it's going to be worth it when I'm done working on it. I told Chandler that I needed at least two weeks to work on the house, so plan the wedding sometime after that. If the house isn't ready, I'll go ahead and move in with him at his place."

"I'll start on the planning as soon as you leave."

"Are you sure your boss won't mind that you aren't doing your work?" she asked teasingly.

"If he does, I'll just complain to the President."

She couldn't believe her sister enjoyed working this closely to her family. "Mariah, don't you find it hard working here?"

"How do you mean?" she asked, confused to what her sister was referring.

"Chandler is your boss, Evan is the President of the company, and Casey is in and out all the time. One's your husband and the other two are your brothers-in-law, doesn't that ever bother you?"

She laughed. "It won't matter in another few months since I'll be quitting to stay home with the baby, but it hasn't been hard. Chandler is a great boss and I get to see my husband throughout the day." She looked around her, then lowered her voice. "Occasionally, we're able to get in a nooner," she said, then laughed, embarrassed by what she had told her sister.

"Mariah!" Whitney exclaimed. "You've done that here at work?"

"Evan has a comfortable couch in his office."

Whitney shook her head. "I don't think I want to hear any more. As it is, the next time I see Evan, I'm going to be thinking about this conversation."

"At least it got your mind off you and Evan." Whitney gave her a strained look and Mariah laughed. "Maybe after you and Chandler have had sex, you can tell me about it." When she saw Whitney's blush, she knew that they had already been intimate. "I take it by your face that you have, and since you're going to marry him, I'll assume it was good."

"Mariah! I'm not going to talk to you about my sexual experience with your brother-in-law."

"Not even to tell me if Chandler's as big as Evan told me he was."

Whitney stood; her face covered in a dark pinkish hue. "I think this conversation has gone too far." At the time they had made love, she had been too occupied with his lovemaking to notice Chandler's size, but now she wondered about it. Was he larger than the average man was? She couldn't compare him to Evan since she didn't remember anything about that night, and she wasn't about to ask him about it.

Mariah reached out to grab Whitney's hand. "I apologize, I shouldn't tease you like this. It's just that I really don't have any close girlfriends, and now that you and the twins are back in my life, I feel I have someone I can confine in about this kind of stuff."

Whitney move to Mariah and pulled her into a hug. "It's okay. I'm just uncomfortable about talking to you about sex. I've had sex with three different men, I was raised that this sort of behavior is wrong, and I felt guilty for what I've done."

"I understand, but I don't think badly of you because of it."

"Thanks, that means a lot to me."

They said their good-byes, then Whitney drove to back to her apartment. As she thought about her new home, she decided that the first thing she needed to do was to empty the yard of the old cars, and so she started looking in the yellow pages until she found someone for the first project. She dialed the number, then waited impatiently for someone to answer, smiling when someone finally did.

"Hello. Gary's Vintage cars. This is Gary, may I help you?"

"I hope so. My name is Whitney O'Rourke. I've bought a property that has thirteen old cars on it. I need to get rid of them and was wondering if you might be interested in them."

"Do you know what year they are?"

"No, but I would guess they're from somewhere between the twenties and thirties."

"Do you have an amount you want for them?" he asked excitedly.

"I wouldn't have a guess. I'm not even sure if they're even salvageable."

"Give me your address and I'll go check them out."

"I'll meet you there." Whitney quickly gave him the information to the house, then left to meet him at the house. As she waited for Gary to show up, she walked around the house, taking pictures of the yard, porch, and the house, as she wanted documentation of everything so she could show Chandler how the place had looked before she started redoing it. She had just returned to the front porch when she saw Chandler drive up into the driveway. A sinking feeling filled her as she watched him get out of the car with a disgusted expression. This was not a good sign, she thought.

"Whitney, do you want to explain this?" he asked, spreading his arms to indicate the entire front yard.

"You promise you wouldn't see the house for two weeks," she said weakly.

"I thought you meant the inside of it. I had no idea you didn't want me to see the outside either. Now I know why you didn't want me to see this junk yard. I'm guessing the inside isn't much better."

Whitney stood in front of the door, preventing him from entering. "You said you'd give me two weeks. Come back then and I'll let you inside."

"Whitney, I can't afford to pay good money for this run-down dilapidated pit. I want you to call the realtor and tell him we've change our minds."

"We've already signed the papers. Besides, I want this house," she said forcefully.

"I don't," he hollered, giving her a stern look.

"Fine, then I'll buy the house myself." She knew as soon as she said it, there wasn't any way she could afford to buy this house.

"How do plan to do that?" he taunted, knowing she didn't have the money to buy any place on her own, let alone this one.

"I'm not sure, but I'll find a way to reimburse you the money you invested into it." She sure hoped she could do just that with the money Gary would give her for buying the old cars. She turned towards the door, but stopped to turn back to him, then she slid her engagement ring off her finger and handed it to him.

He looked down at the ring in his hand, then looked back at her. "Why are you giving back the ring?" he asked, even though he had a dread feeling in the pit of his stomach that she was calling off their engagement.

"I've changed my mind about us."

Chandler reached out to stop her. "You don't mean that!" He yelled angrily at her.

"Getting married was a stupid idea anyway. We don't know anything about each other. You were only marrying me because . . ." she couldn't continue, her tears preventing her from completing her sentence. "Never mind."

"Whitney, please don't do this!" He reached out to grab her hand. "Don't let a house come between us."

"Go away," she insisted, refusing to look at him.

"If that's what you want," he replied sadly.

"It is." She opened the door, hurried inside, slamming the door closed before she could become hysterical in front of him. As she leaned against the door, she let the tears fall, madder at herself for what she had just done than she was at Chandler for not wanting the house. If only she had kept the engagement ring and hadn't said what she had to him, then maybe they could have worked through this, but not now.

It was a good thing she hadn't given her notice at work yet, otherwise she would be in more trouble than she already was. When she heard his car start up, she peeked outside and watched as him drive away, taking her heart with him. She remained standing there looking out the window until she saw an unknown vehicle drive up, then she wiped her tears way, and stepped outside to greet her guest.

"Hello. Are you Gary?"

He put his hand out. "Yes, I'm Gary Elder." He noticed her tears but didn't comment on them.

"I'm Whitney O'Rourke," she said, putting her hand out to him. "I'll hope you have good news for me."

"From what I can see from here, I think you and I can do business," he said, giving her a happy grin.

"There is another vehicle out back in the barn and it's in better shape than any of these."

Twenty minutes later, Whitney had a check in her hand, surprised the old cars had been worth anything at all. The check was large enough for her to reimburse Chandler, pay off the mortgage, and still have some money left over for the things she wanted to do to the house. She went to the bank to deposit her check, and then had a cashier check made out to reimburse Chandler, plus a little extra for interest. Then she went to the post office to mail the check to him, as she was afraid to face him, thinking her heart would break if she did.

She returned to her apartment and picked up the yellow pages again to find a carpenter to demolish the porch and install a new one. She was tickled when she found out that he could also redo the floors and remove the old wallpaper but was especially thrilling that he could get started on her house the first thing tomorrow morning.

She had just laid down to take a nap when her phone rang; she looked over at it but didn't answer afraid it might be Chandler. When she heard Mariah's voice leaving a message on her machine, she quickly picked up the phone. "Mariah, I'm here."

"Are you okay?" she asked carefully.

"I'm fine. Why do you ask?" she asked as her tears started, even though she knew the answer to Mariah's question.

"Chandler stopped by my desk and told me what happened." Mariah waited, but Whitney didn't respond to her statement. "Aren't you going to talk to me?"

"What can I say that he didn't already tell you?" Her tears made it hard to talk.

"Maybe why you bought that house, or maybe why you broke off your wedding."

"I don't have to justify myself to you," she replied tearfully. "It isn't as if we're in love. He just wanted to marry me because of the baby."

"Whitney, you know it's more than that," she insisted, trying to give her sister some comfort.

"I don't know any such thing," she lied, knowing that she and Chandler did have something special. "I'm sorry, but I don't want to talk about Chandler or our relationship."

"Call me if you want to talk."

"Thank you." She hung up the phone, lay back down, and cried herself to sleep.

* * *

Two days later Chandler was going through his mail, when he came across an envelope with Whitney's name on the return address, and he quickly opened it. When he pulled out the check, he let out a loud swear word. He didn't know how she could come up with this amount of money, but he knew he had to find a way to get back into her good graces. For he'd found out recently that his life was empty without her in it.

CHAPTER SIXTEEN

Whitney stood in the driveway admiring her new home, waiting for her lunch date to arrive. Everything was done except for some landscaping, and she planned to take care of that part after lunch today with her realtor. She was wearing a new maternity dress, which hid her small baby budge. She wasn't trying to hide the fact she was pregnant but hadn't planned to say anything to Jack regarding her current condition since after today; she didn't plan to see him again.

He pulled into the driveway, stopping just behind her, and got out.

"Jack, I'm glad you could make it today."

"Well from what I can see so far, I think I lost the bet," Jack said, looking over the place. Then he looked over at Whitney, and saw she was glowing, and naturally assumed the cause of it was the man in her life. When he happened to look down at her hand, he immediately noticed her engagement ring was gone, then quickly thought that maybe it was the fact he was there that was causing her to look so radiate. Maybe he could ask her out, as he'd love to get her into bed and make love to her.

"Wait until you see inside." Excited to show off her new home, Whitney hadn't noticed his intense glance at her hand. "Come in and I'll give you the grand tour."

They entered the house and she proudly showed him around, animated as she bragged about all the work done on the house. She was so excited about the house and its transformation that she still didn't notice Jack's interest in her.

"So, what do you think?"

"You've done a magnificent job. I'm very impressed with all you've accomplished in such a short time."

"Thank you, but I didn't do it myself, I hired great help."

He looked around him. "Why are all the rooms still empty?"

"Because I still need to buy furniture."

"Don't you have any from your apartment?"

"No, it's a furnished apartment."

Jack's first thought was the master bedroom needed a king-sized bed, then they would have plenty of room to romp around when he made love to her. "Well if you need any help with anything, just let me know," he told her seductively, then reached over and took hold of her hand.

Whitney stared at him, surprised when he took her hand. "I'm hungry. Are you ready for lunch?" she asked, quickly pulling her hand away from his on the pretense of picking up her purse.

"Sure," he replied, giving her a confused look.

Whitney was nervous about sitting next to Jack in the car, confused to why he had taken hold of her hand the way he had earlier. She turned to look at him as he helped her into the car, but quickly looked away when she saw him looking down at her bare legs. She wished now that she had worn pants, but she hadn't realized Jack was interested in her. Maybe she should cancel this luncheon, but before she could speak, he started the car.

She was so on edge thinking about this luncheon that she didn't take much notice on where they were going until they were pulling into the Olive Garden's parking lot. Panic filled her as she thought of the Italian restaurant's cozy atmosphere and knew this was the last place she would want to be with this man.

"Jack, would it be all right if we went across the street to Pizza Hut. I really don't care for this restaurant," she told him honestly.

"You don't?" he asked, surprised by her announcement. "I though everyone loved their food."

She gave him a weak smile. "Not me. I rather have home-made Italian food."

"Okay," he replied disappointedly. He had been planning on ordering a bottle of wine with their meal, hoping to loosen her up.

"Thank you, she said, then quietly let out the breath she been holding. Whitney tried to keep their conversation on the house and away from anything too personal, especially to the fact she was pregnant.

Gary's phone rang just as they were finishing their meal, and he took take the call. When he hung up, he told her they had to leave, and she was relieved. When they arrived back at her place, Whitney got out and thanked Jack for lunch. He asked her out for a date, but she said she wasn't interested in getting involved with anyone right now. He told her he would call her in a few weeks, she smiled and told him good-bye.

She hurriedly slammed the door closed, stepped away from the car, and waved, relieved when she saw the last of his car go down the street. She drove back to her apartment to change her clothes, then she went to the local nursery to pick out several varieties of flowers to plant. When she returned to the house, she started planting her flowers. Enjoying being outside, she didn't mind how hot the day had become.

Chandler stopped the car in front of Whitney's home. As he looked around the yard, he was pleasantly surprised to see it completely clean of the old cars and there was fresh sod where the old cars had once sat. He looked over at the house to see it had a new porch and a fresh coat of paint.

If he hadn't seen the yard full of cars and the horrid condition of the outside of the house for himself, he wouldn't have ever believed this property was the same place. From where he sat, he saw Whitney working in her flowerbed. He got out of the car and slowly walked to where she was squatted down in the dirt.

Whitney heard a noise and looked up to see Chandler walking towards her. She stood and brushed off the dirt on her hands. "Hello. What brings you here today?" she asked, trying to keep the excitement of seeing him out of her voice.

He smiled at her appearance, as she had a streak of dirt on her cheek and sweat was running down her face, but to him she looked wonderful. "The place looks great. You've done a great job with it."

"Thank you. What are you doing here?"

"I want to talk to you about the check you sent me."

"There isn't anything to talk about," she replied coolly, as the last thing she wanted was to argue with him.

He decided to try a different tactic. "I thought maybe you would like to go for a stroll with me." He smiled when her expression changed to one of surprise.

"It's ninety degrees out and you want to go for a walk?" She knew he was up to something but didn't have an idea of what it could be.

"I would think it would be less strenuous than what you've been doing," he teased.

Whitney laughed. "You got me there."

He looked at her dirt-covered hands. "Why don't you use gloves?"

"Can't stand the things."

"How about it? Will you go for a walk with me?"

"Let me wash my hands and then I'll be ready. Do you want to come in while I clean up?"

"Sure," he said, then reached over to brush the dirt from her face.

She jerked back when his fingers contacted with her face, as his touch had caused an unsettling fire in the pit of her belly. They walked up the steps to the porch, Chandler opened the door for her, and they moved into the cool house.

"I'll just be a minute."

"Okay." He watched her leave and then looked around the room, seeing that the interior looked as great as the outside had, he could hardly wait for a tour. When she returned from the bathroom, all he could do was stared at her, thinking of how much he would like to take her to bed instead of a walk, and he smiled at the thought.

She saw him staring at her with a sexy grin, and blushed. "Why are you staring at me like that for?" she inquired, wondering if he'd missed her as much as she had missed him.

"I've missed you," he said, taking her hands into his.

"Chandler, please don't do this." She wasn't sure if she could stand for him to touch her, only to reject her.

He quickly removed his hand, afraid he'd scared her, and that was the last thing he wanted to do. "I'm sorry for anything I said badly about the house. You saw its potential when I didn't. Will you show me around?"

She hesitated for a few seconds, then nodded. "Okay."

She walked him through the house, pointing and explaining what she planned to do with each room. When they arrived in the master bedroom, she became uneasy, but she didn't know why. Maybe because it was a bedroom and couples usually had sex in bedrooms.

"I haven't decided exactly what I want in here."

"I have the perfect bed at my place," he said softly, his eyes watching her as he waited for her response.

Whitney fought her tears of regret for her rash decision in throwing their relationship away, but she thought it was for the best. "Chandler, I think it's time for you to leave."

"Damn it, Whitney," he shouted at her, then he grabbed her and pulled her roughly into his arms. "You're mine and I'm not going to let you go." His lips came down hard on hers, then quickly softened as his lips began to make love to hers. A few minutes later, he pulled away from her. "If I don't stop now, we'll end up making love on the floor."

Whitney sobbed in his arms. "Chandler, what are we going to do?"

"About what?" He was unsure to what she was referring.

"Us."

"We'll get married as we first planned," he said, stroking the side of her face with his hand, hoping she wouldn't tell him to get lost.

"I'm afraid," she muttered against his chest.

"What are you afraid of?"

"Are we getting married for the right reasons?"

"I know how I feel about you, and I know that I don't want to live without you."

"How are we going to explain everything to this child when she gets older?" she asked tearfully.

"Honestly."

"Oh, really," she replied sarcastically as she moved away from him. "Hey, honey, the man you've thought was your father for the past ten years is really your uncle and the man you thought was your uncle is really your father because I had sex with my sister's husband. How did that sound?" she asked tearfully.

"Whitney," he said, pulling her back against him. "However, we decide to tell them, I'm sure it can be done in a more delicate way."

"I just think it would be best if we didn't get married. It would be less confusing for the child."

"We'll go talk to a professional, someone who can tell us the best way to tell them. And we are getting married and we're going to do it as soon as possible," he told her forcefully.

His words smoothed her tattered soul. "Okay, if you insist." She gave him a weak grin.

"I do," he said forcefully, returning her grin.

"When should the wedding be?

"Tomorrow?" he asked hopefully.

"Chandler, it can't be that soon. You know Mariah well enough to know she'll have to have at least a week to plan it."

"If it's our wedding, then why should she be the one to plan it?"

Whitney laughed. "Because she's the oldest." Her hand touched the side of his face. "She couldn't keep us together when were little, but now that she's back in our lives, she'll want to make our lives happier."

"I guess we better call her and tell her our news."

"Later, first I want to show you something out back." She took hold of his hand and they walked outside to the barn.

"You want to have sex in the barn?" he asked, squeezing her hand hoping that was the case.

She laughed as she pulled open the door. "I bought this place because of barn. Now you have a place for your horses."

"Whitney," he started, but nothing else came out of his mouth as he took in everything inside the barn.

"I take it you like it," she said, smiling at the expression of joy on his face.

"I can't believe you've done this for me." He turned and pulled her into his arms. "To think I was mad because you bought this place. Thank you, I can't tell you how much this means a lot to me."

"Then show me."

It was sometime later before Whitney called Mariah to make wedding plans. Then she called the twins to tell them the wedding was back on, then lastly, she called her father to ask if he would walk her down the aisle. Erik was touched and agreed to escort her down the aisle.

* * *

As the sisters waited for each of their babies arrival, Lindsay helped Lesley get her book published and it sold like hot cakes. Lesley put some of the profit into accounts for her children's college education fund, and the rest, she and Morgan used for buying whatever they wanted. She started on second book and hoped it would be done before November.

The summer had quickly passed for the four sisters, but by October, time began to slow down for them. Lesley was the most uncomfortable of the four sisters, and swore she was giving birth to two acrobats. Each sister knew the sex of their babies, but the only other person who knew was their husbands and of course, Hailey knew.

Each sister waited impatiently for her big day as November arrived with a severe snowstorm, but no babies. Then the second week went by. On the morning of the third week, the sisters were all starting to get grumpy and short tempered.

When Lesley's water broke, she called her sisters, then they headed for the hospital. Her sisters met them there and stayed with her until the nurse made them leave her room. An hour later, Trace and Trey Clemmens were born, just two minutes apart.

While they waited to hear about Lesley's babies, Whitney went into labor. Whitney had just given birth to her daughter, Lori, when Mariah went into labor.

Mariah's daughter, Reanna arrived just as Lindsay went into labor.

The other three sisters waited together in the waiting room, their babies in their arm as they waited to hear about the birth of Lindsay's baby. Erik held one of the twins while Austin and Nicole were passed between the uncles as they waited for the news of the next Clemmens to be born. The minutes slowly ticked by, then an hour ticked by, but still no baby. Just after midnight, Casey came out to inform everyone that he had a son. Sean had been born two minutes before midnight, making all five babies have the same birthday.

* * *

Two years later, Mariah and Evan had Payton, and Whitney and Chandler adopted five-year-old Dyan, whose parents had been killed in a fire a few months earlier. Lindsay and Casey decided not to have any more children since they had their hands full with Nicole, Austin, and Sean. Lesley and Morgan also decided not to have any more, saying three children were enough for them as well.

EPILOGUE

One day when Reanna, Mariah's daughter and Lori, Whitney's daughter were ten, they were playing at Whitney's house, talking to each other.

"Reanna, you're lucky to have a sister," Lori said with longing.

"Payton is a pain sometimes," Reanna told her cousin. "You should be glad you don't have her as a sister. I wished I had an older brother like you do."

Lori smiled. "Dyan's okay."

"I wish you were my sister."

"Me too, but at least we're cousins. That's almost as good as being sisters," Lori told her as she squeezed her hand and Reanna agreed.

"We look enough alike to be sisters and we have the same birth date, maybe you are my sister."

Lori laughed, and then shook her head. "I don't see how that would be possible. We probably look alike because our mothers look so much alike and our fathers are brothers."

Reanna nodded. "Still, I wish you were my sister."

Whitney just happened to overhear the girls talking and decided it was time to tell them the truth about their relationship, so she picked up the phone and called Mariah.

"Hello?"

"Mariah, it's Whitney. I think the girls are old enough to know truth about them being half-sisters."

"Are you sure you want to tell them?" Mariah asked nervously, as she had hoped they wouldn't ever tell the girls the truth.

Whitney thought back to the day Lori was born. She and Chandler had been alone in her hospital room, Lori was in his arms, and she had the birth certificate application in her hand. "What name should I use for the father on the birth certificate?" she asked, looking over at her husband.

"We should be truthful and use Evan's name. When Lori is old enough, we'll sit her down and explain the situation to her."

"You sure telling her will be a good thing?" She worried that her daughter would think badly of her.

"No, but it has to be done. Every day that we don't tell them, we're living a lie."

Whitney's mind returned to the present. "Chandler told me the day the girls were born that this was something we had to do. They had the right to know, otherwise, we'll be lying to them."

"We'll be over."

"Wait," Whitney called out.

"What?" Mariah asked, wishing her sister would say she'd changed her mind.

"What about Dyan and Payton?" Whitney asked softly. "Shouldn't we tell them too? Have you thought what are we going to do about other children? Are we going to tell them as well?"

"We'll start with the girls, then we'll tell Dyan and Payton. We'll call Lindsay and Lesley, to let them know that we've told the girls, then if they think their children should know, then they can tell them."

Soon the four adults were sitting in Whitney and Chandler's living room alone with Reanna and Lori, while Dyan and Payton played outside. The two girls sat side by side on the couch holding hands, scared that they had something wrong. Whitney assured them that they weren't in trouble, then sat down on the sturdy wooden coffee table in front of them.

"We have something to tell you and thought it was best to do it without Dyan and Payton." She looked over at Chandler for moral support and he smiled at her. She took a deep breath, then started her story. "You remember the story about how Mariah, Lindsay, Lesley, and I were separated where we were younger." The two nervous girls nodded. "What you don't know is that I'd met Evan before I was reunited with Mariah." She looked over at her sister, she nodded, and then she looked back at the girls.

"Evan and Mariah had had a big fight just before he left on a business trip and he thought his marriage was over. On the night I met him, he'd been drinking and when he first saw me, he thought I was Mariah. I told him I wasn't his wife, then sat down next to him as he told me about the woman he loved. By the way he talked about her, I mistakenly assumed his wife was dead and we didn't find out until months later that we were related."

She stopped when she realized she was rambling. "To make a long story, short, he and I . . ." she began, looked at Evan, then stopped. Tears began to form as she stared at her daughter, unsure how she could tell her that Chandler wasn't her father or that she'd had sex with her sister's husband.

"Whitney, let me," Evan said, walking to join Whitney on the coffee table.

"You know how babies are made, don't you?" The two girls nodded. "Sometimes alcohol can make someone do something they normally wouldn't do. On that night that Whitney and I met, we were very drunk, we went to bed together, and together we created Lori," he said quickly.

Both girls gasped and looked over at each other, but Evan continued with his story. "I came home to Mariah and we created Reanna. You two are half-sisters," he said with tears in his eyes, thinking this was the hardest thing he'd ever done in his life.

Lori looked sadly over at the man who she thought as her father. "Does this mean you aren't my daddy anymore?" she choked out.

Chandler hurried to her and pulled her into his arms. "No, sweetheart. It just means you and Reanna are sisters. Nothing is going to change, you'll continue to live with us and call me Daddy, and Reanna will live with her parents."

"Daddy, did you know about me when you married Mom?"

"Yes. She and I met the day she came to tell Evan about you. I proposed to her, telling her that I couldn't have children of my own and I wanted you to be my child."

"Without even meeting me?" she asked with awe.

"Yes, and when Aunt Mariah came into the room and saw your mother, she knew they were sisters, and we have been one big family ever since."

"What about Dyan?" she asked.

"What about him?"

"If you can't have children, who's his daddy?"

"His real mommy and daddy were killed. Your mother and I adopted him when you were about two years old." He watched as her eyes filled with tears up. "Why the tears?"

"Does that mean he isn't my real brother?"

"You aren't related by blood, but he's been your brother in every sense of the word since the day we adopted him. Do either of you girls have any questions?" Whitney asked them, relieved with the two girls shook their heads. "Why don't you and Reanna go play? We'll talk more about this later."

The girls left them, and the four adults looked at each other.

"That went well, don't you think?" Evan asked the others.

"Lori took the news better than I thought she would," Whitney said, looking at her husband.

"Maybe they're too young to understand the significance of the situation," Mariah told her sister.

"With today's television, I'm sure the girls understand infidelity," Whitney said softly, refusing to look at her sister. She took a deep breath, then looked back at Mariah. "After all these years, not once have you yelled at me about that night. I still don't understand how you accepted what I did with your husband as easily had you did."

Mariah hurried over to her. "Whitney, it's like Chandler said about it all those years ago. Evan thought you were me, and you thought his wife was dead, and neither one of you remember that night. It wasn't as if you purposely went to bed together to hurt me. If I wanted to have you both in my life, I had to put that night out of my mind, and I have."

"Don't you think about it every time you see Lori?" Whitney asked her sister, tears running down her cheeks.

"No, I see the daughter of my sister and her husband."

Whitney smiled at her. "Thanks for being who you are. I'm so glad you're my sister and in my life again."

"Me too. You know what I want to do?"

"No, tell me."

Mariah's eyes began to water. "I want to have a professional portrait done of the four of us, like the one we had before our family was torn apart."

Whitney hugged her sister. "I like that idea, but first we need to tell Dyan and Payton about their sisters' relationship."

Mariah took hold of her sister's hand. "Come on, let's do this together."

The two sisters left their husbands behind and went outside to tell Dyan and Payton the truth about the girls. After the children were told, Whitney and Mariah returned to the house with them, both women relieved that the chore of telling the truth about Lori and Reanna's relationship was finally behind them.

The next week the family had their picture taken, and once again, the four Arrington sisters had of picture of them standing side by side. Then they had one with each of their own family alone, and one of the entire family together, which make a wonderful family portrait.

www.ingramcontent.com/pod-product-compliance
Lightning Source LLC
LaVergne TN
LVHW011930070526
838202LV00054B/4574